HIS REJECTION

BY

ANGEL RAYNE

Published by Everblood Publishing, LLC
https://everbloodpublishing.com

ISBN-13: 978-1-945499-73-9

Cover Design by Coffee and Characters

Proofreader: Mackenzie @ NiceGirlNaughtyEdits.com

ALSO BY ANGEL RAYNE

Mafia Romance Reading Order

Luca and Veda

His Game

His Stakes

His Win

Enzo and Sera

His Promise

His Rejection

His Proposal

Stand Alone Novels

Tyler and Ailee

Be With Me

<h1 style="text-align:center">SYNOPSIS</h1>

I'm not a hero. I'll *never* be that guy. No matter how much she makes me wish I could…

My life isn't truly *mine*.

Working for the mafia means my loyalty is to the family. Love and marriage aren't for me.

I can't be what Serafina needs. What she deserves.

But that doesn't stop me from wanting her. From taking her.

From *possessing* her.

She's the only comfort I've known for years. My light in the dark.

And it doesn't matter.

Because keeping her would mean rejecting *everything* else. I can't do that.

So, I'll rescue her from the walking dead man who thought he could take her from me.

But there's nothing I can do to protect her from the monster that's about to destroy her.

Me...

CHAPTER 1

Enzo

Sera has disappeared off the face of the earth as though she'd never existed, and I was about to lose my fucking mind.

She's been gone for a full week now. Luca and Tristan have been working overtime trying to help me find her, and I've never been more appreciative of my friends, or more grateful for the fact that they haven't questioned me once about why I was risking my life—all of our lives—to find her. A woman I barely knew.

What we knew is that Derek Jonak, the walking dead man who took her, seems to have dropped her off at that rundown house and left. She was later picked up by a guy driving an unmarked delivery truck and the house had been cleared out. I'd missed her by less than thirty minutes when I'd arrived.

We'd tracked the truck to the Mexican border, and then we'd lost it.

I paced Luca's office as he spoke with his contact Rene in Mexico, one of the few men he trusted implicitly. They'd mourned the death of Rene's sister together, and Luca had kept his promise to avenge her death by killing the man who'd shot her—Luca's brother Mario—therefore earning him a trusted friend for life, even if they did work on opposite sides of the border.

Veda coming into his life three years later had been a godsend. She'd saved my friend from an emotional spiral of self-destruction. And for that, I will protect her with my life. Always.

"Thank you, Rene." Luca watched me cross the room with impatient strides as he finished up the call. "Yes." He paused. "Yes. Alright. I'll talk to you soon." He hung up the phone.

I stopped on the other side of his desk. "What did he say?"

"He's going to get in touch with some of his contacts throughout Mexico who deal with or who know people who deal with sex traffickers. Maybe someone has seen her. With her pink hair and pierced nose, he's hopeful she'll be remembered."

Nodding, I stepped back. My entire body trembled with the need to hit something. The backs of my legs hit the arm of the couch and I made my way around it and sank down onto the leather cushion. Leaning forward, I braced my elbows on my knees and held my head in my hands.

"Enzo."

It was a command. My head snapped up to find Luca standing in front of me.

"We'll find her."

I nodded again. It was all I could do.

"She's still alive."

"How do you know?" I barely managed to get the words out.

"I know, because they wouldn't have bothered taking her all the way across the border if they were just going to kill her."

A small flare of hope kindled in my stomach. He had a point. I was letting my emotions rule my thoughts.

Sitting down across from me, he mimicked my pose. "I think that guy, Derek whatever-the-fuck-his-name-is, is trying to teach her a lesson. For rejecting him, perhaps. But he's a pussy. He didn't have the guts to hurt her himself, so he sold her."

The office door opened and Tristan walked in, closing it behind him.

Luca and I stood. "Did you find out anything?" I asked him.

He smiled, but it was cold and didn't reach his eyes. "Our boy is in California."

"Do you have an exact location?" Luca asked him.

"I do. And I already contacted Franco in LA and told him we were coming."

We. I was grateful for the support, but I could handle this *stronzo* on my own. "You don't have to come with me. Luca needs you here."

But Luca placed his hand on my arm. "Take Tristan with you. Just in case there's trouble. We don't know why he's in California or what connections he has out there, and our relationship with Franco can be a bit...testy at times."

"What about you? And Veda? Someone needs to watch over you both."

"She's only got one class tomorrow and then she's off for the weekend. I'll take her myself if I need to." He gave Tristan a nod, and he walked out of the office, leaving us alone.

"Luca, you can't be running around out there without protection. There's a target on your head."

But he just put his hand on my shoulder. "I'll be fine. I won't do anything stupid. And I'm trusting you not to leave any evidence that will lead anyone else who happens to be looking for Derek back to us. From what you told me about him, I'm sure we can't be the only ones wanting to shut him up."

I met his blue eyes. "There won't be anything left of him to trace by the time I'm done. And I'll call in Milo to clean up after me."

"Excellent. Be careful." Although I was only slightly taller than him, he took my face between his hands and pulled my head down, kissing me on the forehead. "Keep Tristan near you."

"I will. And I'll be back as soon as I can."

Tristan was waiting just outside the office door when I opened it. "I'll go get the car," he told me.

Luca followed me into the hall. "Call me when it's done. I'll need you both back here by Monday morning."

"I'll have her back by then."

Luca grabbed my arm as I went to leave. "Enzo."

"Yeah?"

"When you get Sera back, be careful with her. I'm sure she's been through a lot, and it'll take some time for her to adjust."

My blood turned to ice at what he was subtly suggesting. But I knew he was right. The chances that Sera had gone untouched this long were nonexistent. "Of course."

He looked out toward the hall, and I could see the concern on his face.

"What is it?"

His blue eyes met mine, and there was regret there. "I don't know much about your relationship with this girl, but we *will* have to tell her father she's here. At some point."

I ground my teeth together until my jaw ached. He was right. We couldn't hide her forever. And yet, I couldn't bear the thought of sending her back there so she could be married off to the highest bidder.

"Enzo."

"I know." My voice was terse. "I know," I said more evenly.

Luca stared at me for a moment. "We'll talk when you get back and figure things out."

I nodded and pulled my sunglasses out of my inside jacket pocket. "I'm going to run by the hotel and grab some clothes. I'll let you know when we leave the city." Leaving him to his work, I went to find Tristan.

At the hotel, I changed into a long-sleeved black shirt, a pair of black cargo pants, and black boots with thick soles. Tristan did the same with the clothes we'd stopped and gotten for him on the way. Forty-five minutes later, we were boarding a private plane to LA.

CHAPTER 2

Enzo

Derek Jonak was staying at a ritzy hotel in downtown Los Angeles under an alias. But I knew his face, and within two hours of arriving Tristan and I were following him toward Pasadena.

"He's pulling over."

"I got him." For someone who was trying to stay under the radar, Derek's bright yellow rental car stood out like a beacon as he pulled off at a Whole Foods and went down into the covered parking lot. Or maybe he wasn't trying to hide. Maybe he had actual business here and was too fucking full of himself to realize who he was messing with when he took a girl like Sera. Maybe he thought he was above any kind of punishment because he made so much money. But money wasn't going to save him this time. I didn't care jack shit about his wealth. No amount of money would make her any less important to me.

I pulled in behind him and waited until he parked, then slowly pulled the loaner SUV up in front of his car so it would be directly in his path. Turning on the blinker, I pretended to wait for a space to open up.

Derek locked his car, checked his hair in the reflection of the window, then walked toward the side of our vehicle.

"Not yet," I told Tristan as I watched him approach from the corner of my eye. "Not yet...now!"

Opening the back door from where he was crouched on the floor, Tristan grabbed two handfuls of Derek's sports coat and dragged him into the backseat. "Got him. Let's get out of here," he said over the shouts of injustice coming from our new passenger.

I was already driving away as Tristan reached over our guest and pulled the door shut. My hands shook with the urge to turn around and wrap them around his throat and squeeze until his face turned purple and his eyes popped out of his head. But that wouldn't help me find Sera. Between his shouts for help, I heard the soft click of a bullet sliding into the chamber.

In the rearview mirror, I saw Derek stiffen, his eyes on the barrel of the gun three inches from his face. "What the fuck is going on? Who the fuck are you?" Even with the threat of a weapon, he still sounded like a pompous asshole.

"Here you go." I tossed Tristan the zip ties I had on the passenger seat.

"Turn around and give me your hands," Tristan told him. His voice was deceptively calm, and much more frightening than if he had yelled.

"Tell me who the fuck you are," Derek ordered. "This is kidnapping. And assault. I have people who'll be looking for me. You're both going to spend the rest of your lives in prison for this."

"You'll find out soon enough," Tristan told him. He was deliberately keeping his attention off of me. "Now turn the fuck around or I'm going to shoot you in the head and splatter your brains all over that window." Always blunt and to the point, Tristan stared him down.

It only took a few seconds before I saw Derek give and turn around so Tristan could secure his hands. "Thank you," Tristin told him when he was finished. "Now do me a favor and sit there and keep your mouth shut, and you might actually make it all the way to our destination alive."

The destination he spoke of was to head east out of the city on a lonely stretch of the Angeles Crest Highway. Somewhere along the way, I was going to pull off the road and interrogate this fucker until he told me who he'd given Sera to. And then I was going to rip him apart with my bare hands and bury the pieces.

Surprisingly, he did as Tristan asked, keeping his mouth shut even as Tristan searched his clothes. He smashed his cell phone and threw it out the window. Any identifying cards he kept. Throwing them out the window would only lead the authorities to what would be left of his body.

"Are you going to kill me?" Derek asked.

Neither of us answered.

"I have money," he told us. "Lots of money. Just tell me your price and I can get it for you."

Again, we kept silent. He tried a few more times before he realized he wasn't going to get a response from us, nor could we be bribed. When he finally understood, he started to sweat, his eyes skittering crazily around the interior of the SUV as he tried to find another way out of his predicament.

We'd been driving for about an hour or so when I pulled off the road and drove down a narrow dirt road hidden between the trees. The area we were in was hilly and covered in trees and scrub brush, providing an easy way for us to get out of sight and hearing range of anyone traveling along the road. While we drove, the searing anger I'd felt had burned through my blood and left only cold ashes behind. I was calm. Collected. And focused on the job ahead.

Tristan dragged Derek out of the car as I pulled on a pair of rubber gloves, then I got out of the car and walked around to the back and opened the hatch. Inside were plastic trash bags, a large plastic drop cloth, and more zip ties. I pulled out the bags and the sheet of plastic and left the zip ties. Let him run if he was stupid enough. I would hunt him down like an animal and rip him apart with my teeth.

When I came around the side of the car, Tristan already had Derek on his knees in the dirt near a large rock. Large enough for us to use as a table as I separated him from his fingers, one by one. I dropped the roll of trash bags and unrolled the drop cloth near the rock. Didn't want to leave any DNA anywhere for the feds to analyze if they happened to come across this spot.

"What are you doing?" Derek asked.

I ignored him, placing rocks on each corner of the cloth to keep it from rolling up. When I was finished, I turned to face him. "I'm giving you one chance and one chance only to answer this question before I torture it out of you. Where is Sera?"

His eyes widened when he saw my face fully for the first time, and I saw a flash of recognition. "I don't know anyone named Sera," he lied.

I smiled, but it didn't reach my eyes. I gave Tristan a nod.

"Get up," Tristan ordered. When he didn't move right away, he jabbed the barrel of his pistol into the side of his head. "Up," he said again. This time he got to his feet, and Tristan walked him unsteadily onto the center of the plastic. "Down." Derek fell to his knees as a terrified sob escaped his lying mouth.

Reaching inside the back of my pants, I took out my gun and laid it on top of the rock. Then I crouched down, lifted my right pant leg and slid my knife out of its holder. It took everything I had to keep my movements slow and controlled when all I really wanted to do was scream my rage into his face as I carved the skin and muscle from his bones slice by slice. But that wouldn't get any information out of him. If I allowed my emotions to come forth, if he saw how desperate I was to get her back, it would give him the power. And that wouldn't get Sera back.

"You took her from the back parking lot of the club where she works." As I talked, I strolled over to him, examining the blade of my knife and testing the sharpness on my thumb. "Does that ring any bells?"

Eyes on the weapon in my hand, he shook his head, keeping his mouth shut for once.

"You threw her into the trunk of your car and took her to a house in San Antonio, where you left her with a group of men. They waited with her until a truck full of woman who had been sex trafficked came to pick her up." Grabbing a handful of his hair, I tilted his head back and pressed the tip of my knife into the pocket beneath his left eyeball. "How about now?" I pressed until I saw a look of panic cross his features. "Do you remember anything now?"

"I don't know what you're talking about," he insisted.

Much as I tried to keep my anger under control, it rose within me, screaming through my blood with renewed force. I ground my jaw together and took a breath. Slowly, and with great pleasure, I sank the knife into the bottom of his eye socket and slid it from the outside to the inner corner as he screamed and tried to jerk his head away, cutting through the inferior oblique muscle. But I didn't remove the eye. Not just yet. I pulled the knife out. "Where is Sera?" I asked him again.

"I don't know!" he cried as he continued to struggle. Tristan knelt behind him, one hand holding his tied hands in place and the other arm wrapped around his neck to hold him still.

"Let me rephrase the question," I told him as I moved my knife to his other eye. "Who did you give her to?"

"I don't know their names!" He was crying fully now.

"What *do* you know, Derek?" I asked him. "Because we're going to stay here all day until I get the information I need."

"She's just a *whore*." He spit out the word, his fear transforming into a false sense of boldness. "She doesn't matter."

Tightening my grip on his hair, I leaned down and put my face in his. "She's the daughter of a mafia man. And she *matters* to me," I told him quietly. Placing the tip of my knife back into the outer corner of his eye socket, I enjoyed the sound of his scream as I slowly and steadily cut through the remaining muscles holding it in place.

A few hours later, I had a name and a phone number, and Derek was missing both eyes, three fingers, all of his teeth, and his tiny dick. I didn't normally enjoy torturing others. Actually, I didn't feel much of anything. It was business. Nothing personal.

But this time...this time I drew it out as long as I could, and I reveled in the pain I inflicted. Downright fucking joy flowed through my veins, increasing with every twitch and scream. Every time he begged for mercy. But before he bled out, I called a friend and had him trace the name and phone number he'd given me to make sure it was legit. Sure enough, it belonged to a man on the FBI's wanted list for human trafficking. "I need everything you have on him."

"Are we done?" Tristan asked.

Ending the call, I slid my phone into the front pocket of my pants. "Not quite."

"Do you want help?"

I stared down at Derek's prone body lying awkwardly on the plastic and shook my head. "No, thank you." Tristan took a few steps back and pulled out his phone to call Luca. Kneeling down on the plastic, I let the rage I'd been holding inside explode inside of me as I finished the job with my bare fists. Then Tristan handed me a boning knife from the back of the SUV.

When I was done, Tristan and I removed our bloody clothes and boots and replaced them with the clean ones we'd brought along. Then we bagged up what was left of Sera's spurned admirer along with our clothes, rolled it all up in the plastic drop cloth, and buried it in front of the large rock. While I double checked the area, Tristan called Milo, our cleaner, and—speaking in code—gave him the exact location of the body. He would take care of it for us. It was safer than driving halfway across the country to bury the body parts.

My phone rang as we were getting back into the SUV. It was my friend with the information I'd asked for, and it was enough to go on.

"Are you sure you want to come with me?" I asked Tristan.

"To Mexico?" Tristan asked.

I nodded.

"Absolutely," he told me. "Let's go get your girl."

My girl.

The words warmed my soul and sent a chill down my spine.

LOVE ALL ANIMAL

CHAPTER 3

Serafina

"*Eres un idiota*! You gave her too much. He likes his girls awake, you *pinche pendejo*."

"Relax. She'll come around in a minute. They always do. Once she's broken in, we won't have to give her as much."

The voices floated around me, rising in volume as the argument progressed—sometimes speaking English and sometimes Spanish. Sometimes a combination of both. I didn't recognize any of them anymore. Not since they carried me out of that first house and threw me into the back of a truck with a group of other girls ranging in age from fifteen to forty. At least from what I could tell, because I'd been drugged. To keep me quiet, I would guess. And it worked. As we drove along, I'd faded in and out of a weird dreamlike state, not sure what was reality and what was a dream.

The trip to where I was now seemed to take forever, and yet no time at all. I don't remember much of it, except that we didn't stop once the entire way. And by the time we got here, the bucket in the corner of the truck was so full of piss and shit it splashed over the sides every time we hit a rut in the road. Some of the girls were too out of it to get up, and laid in puddles of their own waste. They hosed us off like cattle before they brought us into the house.

The feeling of complete and utter terror that kept me paralyzed? I remembered that.

I heard the clink of coins outside of my room as money was exchanged and then the latch of the door. I had no idea how much time had passed, or whether it was day or night. The single window was completely boarded up and heavy curtains hung over it. There was a new voice now. Deep, with a hard accent I couldn't place. "Wake up, woman."

But I didn't want to wake up. I wanted to float in this hazy place in my mind where I didn't feel the stagnant air on my naked skin, and I didn't remember the men that came and went from my new prison.

Sometimes though, they would be late with my next dose and the drugs would begin to wear off, and in these moments, I would claw my way to the surface of my consciousness only to find myself back in the real world surrounded by the overwhelming stench of body odor—mine? Or from the others?—rough hands tearing at my tender skin as I was thrown around on the dirty mattress, my muscles refusing to obey what my mind was trying to tell them. To fight. To run away. To do something other than lay there with words of denial clogging my throat. I didn't like it in the real world. There was only pain and humiliation there. But sometimes, sometimes they were late with my next dose.

And that's when the screams would come.

They simmered within me, starting deep in my gut, then gaining strength as they erupted up through my chest and throat, where they escaped out of my mouth with a force that exhausted me. And yet, I couldn't stop them from coming. Not until the men who kept me here came in with the pills.

In the beginning, I fought them hard, and they would have to hold me down and force them down my throat. But that only lasted the first day or so. Now I was grateful that they gave me a way to escape the horrors of my new reality, and I swallowed them greedily, eager to fall back into the blissful nothingness. To forget where I was and what was happening to me. Or at least be able to endure it until I woke again with only hazy bits of pieces of memories that swiftly faded away. Much like a dream.

Surprisingly though, in those moments when I was conscious enough to wonder if anyone was looking for me, it wasn't my father who came to my mind, the man who raised me. The man I'd known my whole life. The man who needed me so he could marry me off to the highest bidder.

It was Enzo.

The terrifying mafia man who'd promised to save me.

Would he still want me now? In this vortex of time I was lost in, men came and went from my room, too many for me to keep count. Blurry figures with faces that all blended together. Some were more gentle than others, but they all took what they wanted from me. The words of refusal I tried to say coming out as incoherent moans that only spurred them on as they held me down on the filthy mattress that was covered with my own sweat and blood and the secretions of their bodies. My face and body were sticky with it all.

I wished I could fall sleep and never wake up. I wished I could leave this disgusting body.

"Get up, *puta*."

Someone yanked me off the bed, their fingers digging cruelly into my upper arm. "Stop!" I tried to yell, but the word was nothing but a whisper that barely made it past my lips. I didn't know if he even heard me. He stood me on my feet, not giving me time to steady myself before he was dragging me out of the room and into the hallway. As I stumbled along behind him past the doors across the hall, I heard the sounds of headboards slamming into walls and the slap of bodies colliding.

We'd hit the stairs before it came to me that I was still naked. I dug in my heels, trying to stop the forward momentum of his grip on my arm, but instead of stopping, he just gave it a sharp tug. I jerked forward and fell onto my knees, my free hand shooting out to catch myself. I cried out when there was a sharp pain in my wrist, and I tried to scramble to my feet, but I was slow from the drugs and ended up sliding along the floor, feeling like the arm he still held was about to be ripped from my shoulder socket.

When I wasn't moving fast enough, he cursed in Spanish and hauled me to my feet with a look of disgust on his face. I couldn't blame him, really. I smelled horrible, even to myself. Keeping his grip on my arm, he removed his other hand from my sticky skin as soon as he saw I could hold myself up. Then he proceeded me down the stairs.

I kept up with him out of sheer willpower, ignoring the whistles and shouts when we reached the bottom of the stairs and crossed through the main room of the house. Out of the corner of my eye, I saw men lounging around the room, some with women on their laps. Unclothed, like me, with dead, unseeing eyes and slack mouths. I kept my eyes on the scuffed wooden floor, unable to even try to cover myself since the guy taking me out still had a bruising grip on my arm and was walking so fast it was all I could do to keep up with him without falling again.

He took me through a door and out into a small concrete courtyard surrounded by high walls, releasing me so suddenly I stumbled, but I didn't fall this time. It was dark outside, and cold, unlike my stuffy room. But there was enough light from the streetlights behind the house that I could see well enough. My arms crossed over my bare breasts and my right wrist throbbing in pain, I lifted my face, enjoying the fresh air and the breeze that brought goosebumps to my skin. Behind me, I heard water hitting the concrete, but my mind was too fuddled to comprehend what that meant. A second later, ice cold needles of pain were blasting the skin from my back. The spray of water was such a shock, it knocked the air from my lungs.

My immediate reaction was to run away, but there was nowhere to go. Nowhere to escape except back inside the house, and he was blocking my way. Huddled in the back corner of the courtyard, I tried to protect myself as best as I could.

After he sprayed me down from head to toe, he cut off the water and dropped the hose, then picked up a bucket and came over to me. I stared at him through strands of wet hair, watching as he took a soapy sponge from the bucket and dropped it on top of my head. "Wash," he ordered, using his hands to mimic washing his hair.

I blinked at him as suds dripped from the strands of my hair, my thoughts still too convoluted to be able to think clearly. He repeated the motion, and I slowly lifted my arms and put my hands on my head and started to scrub my scalp and hair as he quickly and efficiently rubbed the sponge over the rest of my body, even kicking my legs open and scrubbing me there. There was something dark on the sponge when he finished, and I realized it was blood. I vaguely remembered having pains in my stomach, and I realized now it wasn't because of the men who'd come to visit me. It was because I'd had my period.

Was it over now? Was that why he was cleaning me up? As I had no idea when it had started, there was no way for me to know. But there was an overwhelming sense of relief that my body had chosen this moment in time to clear everything out, as my chances of getting pregnant were reduced since my birth control pills were still in the bag I'd left in my car. Honestly, I'd totally forgotten about them until just now.

Oh my god. What if I'd gotten pregnant?

I tried to think, to figure out how long I'd been here. How long after you stop taking the pill do you become fertile again? I had no idea, but I didn't think I'd been there that long. A week, maybe? Two?

My thoughts were cut off when I was hit with the cold water from the hose again. He rinsed my hair and body thoroughly and then left me shivering in the corner, my teeth chattering, as he wound it back up and left it near the front door. Then he stepped inside the house and came right back out with a dingy white towel in his hands. He gave it to me and I immediately wrapped it around my body, soaking up what moisture I could before I rubbed it briskly over the rest of me, drying my hair as best as I could.

When I was finished, he held his hand out for the towel, but I quickly wrapped it around myself again. "No," I told him with a shake of my head that made the world tilt around me. I was hungry. And thirsty. And I could feel the panic rising inside of me as the drugs wore off. The thought of walking back inside of that house without something covering me making me feel nauseous. "No," I said it again. I knew he understood that word. It was the same in both languages. Besides, he spoke some English.

He sighed heavily, looking at me like he was just so, so tired of dealing with people like me and our foolish demands. Between one blink of my eyes and the next, he was directly in front of me and the towel was ripped from my body. Stepping back, he gestured with his arm for me to go back into the house.

I stood there, swaying on my bare feet with my arms crossed over my front to cover myself, as I tried to remember why I didn't want to go back inside even though I was now fucking freezing. But my brain was still so foggy and I couldn't think. I just knew instinctively that I didn't want to go into that house.

And then I remembered, and the screams began to rise.

But before they could erupt, he cursed in Spanish and looked around real quick as he took my arm and dragged me back inside. Once the door was closed behind us, he pulled me around in front of him and held me tight against his chest as he started yelling orders at a short guy with a shaved head standing in the far corner of the room.

Hands reached out and touched me as he moved me across the room to the stairs, pinching my breasts and grabbing me between the legs as I fought to keep the panic under control. My companion kicked them away. *"No dinero, no mujer!"*

Apparently, they wouldn't be getting any free feels today.

I was back upstairs and in my room in no time at all. The short guy followed us in, a glass of water in one hand and a pill in the other. He shoved them at me and I took them gratefully, swallowing down the drug that would take me away from here. They stayed with me until I stopped shaking and my eyelids got heavy. Slowly, I drifted off into my own world. Even the throbbing pain in my wrist lessened. It didn't take long, probably because I'd barely eaten in days.

As I made my way over to the mattress, I hated the thought of lying on it now that I was somewhat clean, but to my surprise, it looked like it had been flipped over, and a blue bedsheet had been thrown across it. Tears filled my eyes when I saw it, and I gratefully sat down and pulled the sheet up around my shoulders. It smelled musty, but I didn't even care. Leaning back against the wall, I huddled under the thin sheet as I fell into the dream world of my mind.

I don't know how long I was asleep when I was suddenly jolted awake, but it must've been hours, for my hair felt dry and I was semi-aware of where I was, but not to the point where the screams would come. My eyelids were so heavy I could barely open them as I pushed myself up onto one elbow and waited. Then I heard it again.

Pop! Pop! Pop!

My heart began to pound. Was that gunshots? I tried to move, to get off the mattress, but I couldn't make my muscles respond to what I wanted them to do. Silent tears tracked down my cheeks. I wasn't sure if they were from fear or hope. Maybe a little bit of both. It could be anyone down there. A rival gang. A disgruntled customer. Or someone who'd come after one of the other girls. I knew the chances that it was someone my father had sent were few and far between. He didn't even know I was in Austin, so how would he have followed me here?

I heard shouts downstairs and more gunshots. Then a guttural scream that morphed into a wet, gurgling sound. In a rush of panic, I dragged myself off the mattress and over to the corner of the room. There was a spot I'd found there after my first "customer." A floorboard that was loose where two of them connected. Pulling it back as far as it would go, I fought to stay conscious as I squeezed my hand inside, my fingers searching for the items I'd stashed there. A ring. A watch. A money clip. Small items that I barely remembered taking while they were too distracted to notice or that were left in my room. I didn't take something from everyone who entered my room. Most of the time I was too out of it to even realize what was happening until later when I found the evidence on my body. Clutching everything in my fist, I made my way back over to the mattress and curled up under the sheet. I don't know why I felt like I needed to have these things on me, but I was either about to be rescued or killed, and for some reason, I felt it was important.

And then everything went eerily quiet. Cowering in the corner of the mattress, I tried to make myself as small as possible.

The floorboards outside my door creaked, and I heard the door across the hall open. I listened intently as the footsteps faded as the person outside my room made their way down the hall to the other rooms. Maybe it was one of the guys who ran the house, checking to make sure we were all still here now that'd they'd killed whoever had tried to interrupt their business. Or maybe they were all dead. Maybe one of the customers decided he didn't want to pay anymore. Hysterical laughter bubbled up inside of me and I slapped my hand over my mouth, trying to keep quiet.

The footsteps stopped outside my room. I tried to keep my eyes open as the doorknob turned and the door slowly creaked open. Hope flared inside of me, but I dashed it down. No one knew where I was. No one was looking for me...

A gun barrel appeared through the crack in the door and slowly swung around the room until it pointed directly at me. The door was pushed open a little more.

Oh, my god.

A violent sob burst from me before I could stop it.

He'd found me.

CHAPTER 4

Enzo

I immediately lowered my weapon when I saw there was only one occupant in the room. The woman cowering on the mattress was nothing like the confident female who'd shown up at my door in a dress that looked like it was made of nothing but fucking bandages. I almost walked away, thinking I had the wrong room, until I saw a lock of pink hair sticking out from beneath the sheet covering her body and most of her face. "Sera?"

Her sob was raw and painful in my ears, but she didn't move. Didn't come to me. I scanned the room, wondering if someone was in there with her. If it was a trap. But I saw no one. I slid on the safety and shoved my gun down the back of my pants, then pulled out my cell phone and called Tristan.

He answered on the first ring. "Yeah."

"I've got her. Is everything clear outside?"

"You're good to go. I'll meet you at the front door."

He didn't ask if anyone was left alive inside. There was no need to. I ended the call and slid the phone back into my pocket, then stepped fully into the room and closed the door, but didn't latch it. "Sera, baby. It's just me. You're okay." I spoke softly to her as I approached. "It's just me, baby girl. It's just me."

I knelt on the mattress and reached for the sheet with hands that shook with the effort it took me not to rip apart this entire fucking room, this entire house. I wanted to scream and rage that she'd been brought here. That I didn't find her sooner. That I didn't save her. All of the dead bodies littering the place? I wanted to kill them all over again. Only slower this time. But I kept my movements steady, my voice calm, despite the violent anger erupting inside of me. She didn't need that shit from me right now. "It's just me," I repeated. "I won't hurt you."

Her movements were slow and sluggish as I pulled the sheet away so I could see her face. Her eyes were half shut, her mouth slack, as she tried to focus on me and keep the sheet over her at the same time. It took her a few seconds for her eyes to lock onto my face, but when they did, tears ran down her cheeks, and every time she exhaled, she did so on a sob. She smelled like lye. And the mattress she was on smelled like sweat and sex.

"You wanna keep the sheet? That's okay. You can do that," I told her. "But I'm taking you the fuck out of here." I brushed her hair back from her face. "I'm taking you out of here right fucking now."

She clutched the rough material to her chest with her arms still underneath and I wrapped it around her as best I could before I slid one arm around her back and one under her knees and picked her up. She weighed practically nothing as I stood with her. Did the bastards even fucking feed her? Or did they just use women up until they were worthless to them and then bring in the next batch?

As we entered the hall, I tucked her into my chest. "Don't look," I told her. She did as I said, burying her face into my bloodstained shirt as I picked my way over the bodies on the stairs and in the main room. I didn't stop to see what the other girls in the house were doing. They could stay or go as they pleased. They weren't my concern. I wasn't here to play the fucking hero. Just to get Sera back.

Tristan was standing guard at the front door when we arrived. When he saw us coming, he led the way out of the house, gun held casually by his thigh as he watched for anyone who might try to stop us until we reached the car Rene had loaned to us. But no one showed their face.

I slid into the backseat with Sera, and Tristan jogged around the front of the vehicle and got into the driver's seat. I held her tight against me as we drove out of the city to the small airport where Rene was waiting for us to ensure we got out of the country safely. Knowing how dangerous it was for us to be there like this, no one spoke a word until we were back on the private plane.

Even then, I wouldn't let her go.

"What the hell did they give her?" Tristan asked as he took a seat across from us after thanking Rene for all he'd done to help us and promising to give his regards to Luca.

"I don't know," I told him. "If I were to guess, maybe large doses of Molly. But her pulse is strong and her color is decent. She'll be alright. It just needs to wear off."

He nodded, then buckled himself in for takeoff. I knew I should put Sera in the seat beside me and do the same for her, but I couldn't bring myself to even do that much. Besides, she had a death grip on my shirt, and she was completely nude underneath the sheet. I didn't think to look and see if there were any clothes in the house I could've brought for her, but there wasn't time anyway. And I sure as hell wasn't expecting they'd deny her something as decent as clothes.

"I'll call Luca as soon as we're in the air and let him know we're on our way home."

"Ask him to bring her some clothes." I laid my head back against the seat and closed my eyes. It was cloudy outside, and my sunglasses darkened things even more, but I couldn't sleep. Not until we were safely back across the border.

By the time we landed two and a half hours later, my arm muscles were shaky from holding Sera so tight against me. She'd fallen into a fitful sleep on my lap almost as soon as we were seated, and I hadn't wanted to wake her.

"Enzo?" She said my name so quietly I almost didn't hear her, her vocal cords scratchy and raw. But her eyes were open, and she had more muscle control in her face now.

"We're home," I told her. "Can you walk?"

"Probably." But she made no move to get off my lap as Tristan unbuckled his seatbelt and made his way to the front of the plane to pay the pilot. "Thank you for finding me," she whispered, and tears filled her eyes and rolled down her cheeks. "Thank you...for..."

"Shhh. You're welcome," I told her. "I'm taking you to my hotel, and we'll get you cleaned up. Luca is bringing you some clothes."

"Okay." She paused. "Is there a bathroom on this plane?"

"Of course." I lifted her gently off my lap and stood, holding her steady until I knew she wasn't going to fall over. The sheet gaped open in the front, and I ground my jaw when I saw the weight she'd lost.

"I'm sorry," she told me, her eyes on her feet as she tightened the sheet around her again.

"You have nothing to be sorry for," I told her. "Hey." With one hand, I lifted her chin, but she wouldn't meet my eyes. "You have nothing to be sorry for," I insisted. "Do you hear me?"

She nodded, but I could tell she didn't believe me.

The door at the front of the plane was open, and Tristan was already down the steps. I gestured to him that we'd be right down and helped her into the small bathroom near the cockpit. "Do you need help?"

She shook her head.

"Leave the door unlocked," I ordered, worried she'd pass out again. Then I stood in front of it with my arms crossed over my chest until she was finished. She was so weak she could barely hold the door open to get out and I had to help her. "Let's get you back to the hotel." I indicated for her to walk in front of me, noticing the way she flinched at every little noise. I didn't tell her she had no reason to be frightened. That there was no reason for her to act this way anymore. She'd been through a lot of trauma. It would take time for her to come back to the world she'd left behind. And she might never be the person she was before. Not fully.

I understood that. Better than most other people, perhaps. Though maybe not for the same reasons.

When she reached the door, she slowed, and then stopped. She took a step back.

"Sera?"

Turning partially toward me, she whispered, "I don't want anyone else to see me like this. Not...like this."

"Okay." I stepped around her and looked outside, not bothering to remind her that Tristan had been with us the entire time. Two cars were waiting for us. Luca and Tristan stood near the one in front. When Luca saw me, he walked to the bottom of the stairs. "Go on ahead," I told him. "We'll be right behind you."

He didn't question why we weren't coming off of the plane. Tristan had probably filled him in on the condition Sera was in. "Are you coming to the house?"

I heard Sera behind me and reached for her without taking my eyes off of the man who was both my friend and my boss. Her hand slid into mine and squeezed my fingers, hanging on tight. "No," I told him. "I'm taking her to the hotel. For now," I added.

But Luca shook his head. "I don't like it, Enzo. I'd rather you both be at the house. It's safer there."

He didn't have to explain what he meant. Her father knew she was here, and the chances that he'd already sent some of his men to the city were high. "I'll bring her on Monday." I wasn't going to back down on this one. She'd been through enough without adding to it by parading her in front of everyone. "I'm asking for a couple of days alone with her. Then we'll come to the house and figure everything else out."

I thought for a moment he was going to refuse my request, but in the end, he gave me a nod. "I'd feel better if you had Tristan with you."

"There's no need," I told him. "Tris has done enough."

His jaw clenched and he looked away, then back at me. "Alright," he said finally. Pulling out his phone, he called my driver and told him to join them in the first car. "The keys are inside, and there's a blanket and a bag with some clothes Veda sent for her. I'll see you in a few days. But I'll be checking in with you periodically. Keep your phone nearby."

"Of course." I waited until they were both in Luca's car and it had pulled away. "Come on." I wished I had something more to cover her with as we descended the stairs and the wind whipped around us. It felt like more rain was coming.

When I reached the bottom of the steps, I turned around and lifted her into my arms so I could carry her across the asphalt. I shifted her weight into one arm and opened the passenger door, tucking her inside and closing it quickly. Then I jogged around to the other side and got in with her, starting the SUV and turning on the heat before I reached into the back for the extra blanket. It was soft and warm, and I spread it over her. "Better?"

"Yes, thank you," she whispered.

"Luca brought you some clothes. As soon as we get back to the hotel, we'll get you clean."

"It's okay," she said, and her voice shook with emotion. "At least I have this." She moved the sheet a little. "I didn't even have that until today." She frowned. "I think it was today."

Jesus fucking Christ. Throwing the SUV into gear, I headed toward the hotel.

"Enzo?" she said after we'd been driving for a few minutes.

"Yeah?"

"How long have I been gone?"

I glanced over at her, surprised to find her eyes on me for the first time since I'd taken her out of that damn house. And I fucking hated how haunted they were. "A week," I told her. "Seven days." I wanted to ask her details about what happened during that time. I could guess well enough. But a part of me needed to hear it. Needed to know everything she'd gone through. But not today.

"It feels like longer." She turned her head away and stared out the windshield, and both of us fell silent as I pulled onto the highway and headed toward the city. When she did speak again, her voice was hard and cold. "It was the guy from the club. The one who left the bruises on my leg."

"I know," I told her.

Surprised, she asked, "How?"

"Because we went through the video feed at the club and saw him put you in his car." I paused. "And because he confessed it to me before I killed him."

She went back to staring out the windshield. "I hope it was painful."

"It was," I told her. "Very."

"Good," she said after a moment.

She fell quiet again, and I wished more than anything that I could hear what was going through her head.

"We're here," I said as we pulled into the drive in front of the hotel. "Stay where you are. I'll be right back." Getting out of the vehicle, I met the valet around the front of the car. It was the young guy with the blond hair, but I'd always gotten a good vibe from him. He seemed mature for his age.

He met me with a smile, eyes carefully averted from the blood on my shirt and jacket. "Good evening, Mr. Delligatti."

"Good evening. I need you to clear out the lobby for me."

To his credit, he disguised his surprise. "Clear out the lobby, sir?"

"Yes. Go inside and tell the front desk I need the entire lobby emptied." I offered no explanation, and he knew better than to ask for one.

"Yes, sir. Give me one moment." Turning on his heel, he walked briskly inside, stopping only to say something to his partner at the valet stand. She glanced up at me and followed him.

Two minutes later, he was back, and he was alone. "The lobby has been cleared, sir."

"Thank you," I told him, and handed him my keys and a wad of cash. "Please turn around and wait for me and my guest to get inside before you park the car. Then bring the bag in the backseat up to my room and leave it outside the door."

"Yes, sir."

He did as I asked, and I walked over to the passenger side and opened the door for Sera. "Watch where you're walking. Do you want me to carry you?"

"No," she said. "I'm okay." But she didn't immediately go into the hotel. "Thank you," she whispered, and there were tears in her eyes. "Again."

"Come on," I told her. Wrapping my arms around her and the thick blanket, I helped her inside, my senses on high alert the entire time. I heard a car door close behind us when we were about halfway through the lobby. True to his word, the valet had completely emptied it. Even the desk clerks were gone.

Sera was quiet as we took the elevator up to my room. And as I opened the door, I could sense her hesitation as she stood just outside, staring into the small foyer. "Sera?"

She made no move to enter.

"Sera, let's go inside."

I was beginning to wonder if I was going to have to carry her in there when she took a shaky breath and crossed the threshold. I followed her in, shutting and locking the door behind us. Out of the corner of my eye, I saw her flinch when she heard the click of the deadbolt. "I have to lock it. Because of who I am."

"I know," she answered. "It's okay."

"As soon as the valet brings the bag of clothes up, I'll go get us something to eat. You can take a shower if you'd like."

She nodded.

"I'll be right back." I went into my room and stripped out of my bloody clothes, throwing on a pair of jeans, a plain blue T-shirt, and running shoes. I buckled on my shoulder holster and covered it with a loose black hoodie that zipped up the front. Picking up my keys and my wallet, I put them in the pockets of my jeans. I grabbed my sunglasses last.

When I came back out, I found her exactly where I'd left her. "Sera?"

Her eyes flew to my face like I'd caught her doing something she shouldn't.

"What's going on?" I asked her.

At first, she didn't respond. Her beautiful eyes flicked away and she frowned, like she was struggling with something.

"Whatever it is," I told her, "you can tell me."

Her eyes found me across the room. "If I asked you to kill someone for me, would you do it?"

"Yes," I told her without hesitation.

"What if it was more than one person?"

"Yes," I said again. And at that moment, I knew I would, without hesitation.

Her arm moved beneath the sheet and her hand appeared, closed into a fist. Slowly, she opened her fingers.

I stepped closer, wanting to see what she was showing me. Lying on the palm of her hand was a man's ring, a watch, and a money clip. "What is this?"

Her voice was little more than a whisper. "These belong to men who came to the house. Men who hurt me." She held them out, and I opened my hand so she could dump them into my palm. "I couldn't get something from everyone, but I got these."

I knew then what these were. She'd stolen them from men who had fucked her. Hurt her. And now she wanted me to find them and kill them. I raised my hand closer to my face. The ring had a crest on it. One that I recognized. The money clip was engraved with initials. But the watch didn't give me anything to go by. Even so, I put it into my pocket with the rest. "What would you like to eat?"

"I'm not very hungry."

"I understand, but you need to eat something. Pizza? Sandwiches? Soup?"

She thought about it. "Soup sounds okay."

"Good. I'll bring the bag inside and leave it on the bed for you. Will you be okay for a few minutes? I'm just going to run downstairs."

She nodded.

"I'll be right back," I told her. Watching her, I didn't want to leave. She looked like she was barely holding it together. "Sera."

Her eyes found my face, met mine.

"I'll be right back," I repeated. "You're safe here."

She nodded again. "I think I'll take a shower."

I heard someone outside the door and opened it to find the bag of clothes Luca had brought. I put it in on the bed for her, then approached her cautiously, watching her eyes. "I'll be ten minutes," I told her. Unable to keep myself from touching her, I cupped her cheek in my hand and ran my thumb over her lush bottom lip. She stood stiff and still as I did so, wide eyes on my face. "Ten minutes," I repeated. Against my better judgement, I left her to get cleaned up.

The items in my pocket jingled against each other as I walked out to the elevator. A death knell for every man that laid so much as a finger on her without her permission.

I would keep my promise to her.

I would find them and I would kill them all.

LOVE ALL ANIMAL

CHAPTER 5

Serafina

It won't come off. That feeling of other people's hands on me. Men's hands. Their spit. Their semen. No matter how hard I scrub at my skin, it won't fucking come off.

"Shit. Sera! What the fuck are you doing?"

I jumped when I heard Enzo's voice. "I can't get clean." Desperately, I looked up at him through the clear glass door of the shower. "I can't get clean!" My voice rose in panic.

He opened the door and grabbed my unhurt wrist, stopping my frantic movements. "What the fuck is this? What *is* this?" Wrestling the loofah out of my hand, he brought it to his nose. "What's on here?"

I started to cry as he searched the bottles in the shower until he found the bleach cleanser I'd found under the bathroom sink that I was now using as soap.

"Get under the water," he ordered as he took off his shoes and socks.

"But I'm not clean!"

"Under the fucking water, Sera." Fully clothed in jeans and a T-shirt, he got into the shower with me, taking up so much space he forced me to move back under the spray.

"I'm not clean," I sputtered as the water rushed over my head and down my face and body.

"You're not dirty," he ground out, and I looked up to find honesty in his dark eyes. "Sera, you are not dirty." But no matter what he believed, he was wrong. I would never feel clean again. And it had nothing to do with how many times I showered.

I felt the screams begin to rise inside of me and I tried with everything I had to suppress them, to think about something else. I was here now, with Enzo. He wouldn't let anything happen to me. Not again. I wasn't in that house anymore. I was back in Texas. In Austin. Enzo had saved me. Everything was okay.

It didn't work. Like a volcano that had lain dormant for too long, they pushed and swelled inside of me until they were leaking through the seam of my lips, no matter how hard I tried to keep them inside.

"Sera, look at me. LOOK at me."

Desperate now, I pressed my lips tighter together and found his eyes. They locked onto mine and wouldn't let me go.

"You're not in that house anymore. You're with me. You're safe." His voice was low and soothing, and I concentrated on what he was telling me. "Part of what's going on with you is that you're coming down off the drugs they gave you, and things might be a little crazy until they wear off completely. That's to be expected when they're given to you so consistently for so many days in a row."

I had no idea if that was true or if he was feeding me a bunch of bullshit, but I hung onto his words like they were a lifeline.

"Are you hearing me?"

I nodded my head and tried to answer him, but I was afraid to open my mouth. He took my face in his hands and kept talking to me. He pointed out things for me to look at, things for me to touch, placing my hands on his chest over the wet fabric of his T-shirt. Kissing the palms of my hands. The inside of my wrists until the panic inside of me began to subside.

I flinched when he innocently twisted the one my captor had yanked on. Enzo caught the movement and stilled. "Are you hurt?"

"Just my wrist," I whispered, trying to hold it up.

A murderous rage came into his expressive eyes as he eyed the developing bruises. "Who did that to you?"

"It was just an accident."

"Did you fall on it?"

Unable to look at him, I shook my head. I hadn't fallen. But I don't think he'd meant to hurt me.

"Someone hurt you." It wasn't a question.

"It was an accident," I repeated. "I don't think he meant to do it. He was just trying to get me up, and the drugs..." I trailed off.

"Who was it, Sera?" His voice was deceptively calm.

"I didn't know his name, but I think he's dead now," I told him, and frowned. "I think you killed him." I paused. "He never really hurt me before. Not that I can remember. He worked in the house. Dealt with the..." *Rapists.* "... customers. But I'm still glad he's dead."

He didn't say anything for a really long time. Beneath my palms, I could feel his body vibrating with anger that I wasn't capable of feeling yet, although I'm sure it would come. However, right now, I couldn't feel anything other than the residues of panic. Leaving my hands on his shirt, he rubbed my upper arms. "How you doing?"

"I'm not sure."

"You're still shaking," he told me. Then he suddenly changed the subject. "Tell me about what your life was like growing up."

I frowned. "W-What?" My skin burned where I'd scrubbed myself and his hands hurt where he touched me, but I felt like he was the only thing keeping me from falling down the spiral of my hysteria.

He picked up the bottle of shampoo and squeezed some into his palm. "Growing up. I wanna know what you were like when you were a little girl." Lathering it up in his hands, he started washing my hair. "What's your natural hair color?"

"My hair?" I was having a hard time keeping up with the conversation. I tried to concentrate on what he was saying.

"Yeah, your hair. Is it blonde? Red? Brown?"

"Um..." I tried to think back. "It was really light when I was little. But then it turned kind of dishwater blonde when I was a teenager."

"How long have you been coloring it?"

My eyes closed as his strong fingers massaged my scalp. "I didn't. Not until I came here."

"And you chose pink. Lean your head back."

I did as he told me, grateful to have someone else take over the task of washing me because it was everything I could do right now just to keep my panic in check. "I like pink."

"I like pink, too," he said quietly. "Especially on you."

Once the shampoo was rinsed, he conditioned my hair as I stood there like some kind of broken doll, moving only when he directed me to do so. The entire time, he talked, keeping me distracted and not allowing my mind to wander too much. He asked me questions. Told me stories about things he and his friends had done when they were younger that sounded too outrageous to be real.

"Your clothes are getting wet."

He blew off my concern. "They'll dry," he said.

I looked at this man, a man I barely knew, really. A man who was hard and dangerous. A killer. And yet, here he stood in the shower with me as I fought not to break into a million pieces, taking care of me. He'd found me all the way in Mexico. And not only that, he'd come after me himself and brought me home. I knew he'd killed everyone who was in that house, and I didn't care. I was glad.

What kind of person did that make me?

"Ready to get out?"

I blinked, pulling myself from my thoughts. "Yeah." The water was starting to cool down, and I shivered.

Enzo reached around me to shut off the water, and I inhaled his dark forest scent, already so familiar to me. It smelled like home.

I was home.

Out of nowhere, I burst into tears.

"Hey, hey. What's this?"

"I'm s-sorry." I tried to get control of myself, but all I could do was stand there, naked and cold, with my wet hair hanging over my face as violent sobs wracked my body.

Without another word, Enzo opened the shower door and grabbed a white towel off the towel rack. He let me cry as he dried me off, starting with my hair and then working his way down my body. Despite his previous aggressive behavior toward me, I didn't feel nervous or threatened.

I felt...cared for.

When I was wrapped in the large towel, he held my hand and helped me step out of the shower. Then I waited as he pulled off his wet shirt and jeans and threw them back into the shower. In only his wet boxer briefs, he placed a hand on my lower back and led me into the bedroom. "Do you wanna get dressed?"

Sniffling, I nodded my head.

"Okay, why don't you do that while I dry off and take care of my wet clothes. Then we'll eat." Grabbing some dry clothes for himself, he took them back into the bathroom and closed the door behind him, leaving it cracked a few inches. I heard the shower come on again.

On shaky legs, I walked over to the bed and sat down on the edge near the nightstand. There was a box of tissues there, and I grabbed a bunch and blew my nose. Then I used the towel to clean up my face. I felt better. Calmer. I guess losing my shit for a few minutes wasn't necessarily a bad thing.

By the time Enzo came out, with wet hair and in clean jeans and a T-shirt, I was dressed in the T-shirt and yoga pants his boss had brought for me and sitting in the other room. There was no underwear, no bra, but I was okay with that. He'd gotten me butternut squash soup and crusty bread with butter from somewhere, and it was so good it almost made me start crying again. "Thank you for the soup," I told him when he joined me on the couch. He was a big guy, and he made me feel tiny sitting beside him. My eyes felt swollen and my voice was ragged from crying, but the violent urge to scream was little more than a tickle in my gut.

"How's the soup?" Taking the lid off of the other container that was in the bag, he brought it to his nose and sniffed. "Smells good."

"It's the best thing I've ever tasted."

He gave me a look. "I'll bet it is." Then he set his container down on the coffee table and braced his elbows on his knees, hanging his head.

I set my own soup down. "What's wrong?"

It took him a minute to answer me, and when he did, it wasn't what I was expecting to hear. He took a deep breath, and then tilted his head to look at me, and I was struck by the power of emotion in his dark eyes. "I'm sorry," he told me simply. "That it took me so long to find you."

I just stared at him for a moment. "Enzo—"

He cut me off. "No. You were under my protection, and I failed you. And I want you to know that I'm sorry. It won't happen again."

Something stirred deep within my chest. "But you did find me, and you got me out of there. There's no need to be sorry. I'm very grateful to you."

He ran his hands through his hair, making it stick up all over his head even more so than normal. He didn't seem to believe me.

"Enzo, it wasn't your fault. You tried to tell me to stay where I was until you could get to me, and I didn't listen. What happened isn't on you." It was on me. It was all my own fault. I should've listened to him. I should've stayed in my car at the club until the security guard came out to walk me inside. I shouldn't have left my cell phone in my bag. There were so many reasons I could put the blame on myself, and not one where I should put the blame on him.

His voice was gruff. "It won't happen again."

"Okay," I told him.

We sat quietly staring at each other for a bit, silently saying things neither one of us was ready to say out loud, until he broke the silence. "Eat your soup and bread. You've lost too much weight."

Too tired to argue with him, I picked up my container. Once he was satisfied I was eating, Enzo did the same.

"So, what's going to happen now?" I asked him when I couldn't eat another bite.

"We can stay here for a few days. Give you a little time to adjust. On Monday, I have to report back to Luca's and you're coming with me. He has a large house. It's where I stay when I'm not here. And now that he knows about you, I want you there with me where I can protect you and be there if you need anything." He paused, as though he expected me to argue with him. And the Sera he knew before might have done just that. But this Sera really didn't want to be left alone. I also didn't want to go back to Jade's and try to explain everything that had happened. As far as she knew, I was long gone. And it was safer for her to keep believing that.

When he saw I didn't have any objections, he continued. "Once we get to Luca's, we'll discuss what we're going to do about your father."

"Will I have any say in that?"

He paused. "Not much, no."

I almost laughed. I should've known better than to even ask. It wasn't how things were done in the mafia world. A world run by men and their whims, with very few exceptions.

But he must've seen what I was thinking on my face. "I'll do what I can, Sera. But that's all I can promise you."

"I get it," I told him. "But you know that's bullshit. I'm not a child, and it's my life. I should have a say in it."

He got up from the couch and picked up our empty soup containers, putting them back in the plastic bag they came in and setting them outside the door in the hall to be picked up by hotel staff. He didn't argue with me. Didn't try to defend the men he worked with.

And he was right to hold his tongue. There was nothing to argue about. The world of the mafia was the way it was. And me bitching about it wasn't going to do anything to change it.

Coming to stand in front of me, he put his hands in the pockets of his jeans. "It's late, and you should get some sleep."

Again, he was right. I was exhausted. However, the thought of sleep wasn't a comforting one.

"I can sleep out here on the couch," he said.

I felt the weight of his stare on me as I thought about that. Did I want him to sleep out here, leaving me alone in the bedroom? No. I didn't think I did. "No, you don't have to do that."

"It's no problem. And it won't be the first time I've slept on this couch."

But I shook my head. "I don't want to be by myself," I confessed.

He studied me for a long time. "Okay," he finally said. "Then let's go to bed."

I stood up, and rubbed my sweaty palms on the front of my pant legs. "Enzo..." I didn't know how to say what I needed to tell him.

But he just said, "I know. It's okay."

I released the breath I didn't realize I was holding as relief washed over me. I didn't want to be alone, but I also didn't think I was ready for what he would want from me.

"It's okay," he repeated softly. "Let's get some sleep. And we can talk some more in the morning."

I walked ahead of him into the bedroom. Despite his reassurance, I was nervous. "Do you have an extra toothbrush?"

"There's a new one in my travel bag under the sink."

Shutting the door behind me, I found the toothbrush and brushed my teeth. My hair was still damp, so I used Enzo's comb to untangle it. The bathroom smelled like bleach, as did I. The skin on my arms was bright red.

Setting down the comb, I lifted the T-shirt I was wearing. My stomach and breasts were red too. Everything still burned.

Maybe it would burn away a few layers of skin so I wouldn't have to carry their touch with me everywhere I went.

Tugging down my shirt, I finished up and left the safety of the bathroom.

Enzo was sitting on the side of the bed, waiting. When I came out, he stood and came to me. Taking a strand of my hair between his fingers, he rubbed them together. "So soft," he murmured. Leaning down, he pressed a soft kiss to the top of my head. Then he released my hair and went into the bathroom, closing the door behind him.

I got into bed, still fully dressed. Taking a deep breath, I released it on a heavy exhale, feeling some of the tension finally leaving my body as I sank into the soft mattress. The white sheets and gray comforter smelled clean and were soft on my raw skin. I pulled them up around my neck, trying to get warm.

Enzo came out a few minutes later. I watched him walk around the bed so he could sleep closest to the door. He took off his jeans and shirt and laid them on the chair near the window, leaving on his boxer briefs, then he climbed into bed and turned off the lamp beside the bed. Rolling over, he wrapped his arm around me and pulled me into the curve of his body.

My heart sped up, and I stiffened when I felt something long and hard against my ass. "Enzo—"

"Shhh...I just wanna hold you, that's all."

He held me tight against him, his arm heavy on my ribs and his hand spread wide over my chest above my breasts, his fingers on my collarbone. I was sure he could feel my heart racing.

I laid there for a long time, my body strung tight, feeling his hard chest rise and fall against my back with his steady breaths, until I gradually began to relax and my eyes started to grow heavy.

I wasn't sure if I was awake or dreaming when I heard him say, "Don't ever leave me again, Sera."

With a sigh, I sank into sleep until the screams rose inside of me again.

CHAPTER 6

Enzo

A woman was screaming in my dreams, her terror ripping through me as though it were my own.

I flew out of the bed like it was on fire, my hand going immediately to my nightstand drawer where I'd stashed my gun earlier. Before I was even fully awake, I had a bullet in the chamber as my eyes swung around the room, searching for the threat.

But there was no one there except me and Sera, who was lying stiff and still, her face contorted in terror as breathless screams tore from her throat, triggering things inside of me I'd rather not revisit.

My heart began to pound, and my hands started to shake. I broke out into a cold sweat. Sera struggled against the invisible bonds holding her in place, tears flowing down her cheeks. Carefully, I slid the safety on and set the gun down on the nightstand. It rattled as it hit the wood, and I quickly let go of it. Memories of Alessandra and Elliot swept through me, distorting my vision of reality. Concentrating on my breathing, I fought down the panic attack that was threatening to overwhelm me.

Quite a traumatized pair we were.

I knew how to talk her down earlier, and I used those same tactics on myself now. Sera needed me. I didn't have time to give in to this pussy bullshit. So as I climbed back onto the bed, I counted three things I could feel. Three things I could see. Three things I could smell. And when I reached her, I was out of my own head enough to take her by the shoulders and sit her up. "Sera. Baby, it's me. It's just me."

Her head lolled to the side and her eyes rolled back in her head as she tried to fight me off with weak strikes of her fists. I kept talking to her, repeating the same thing over and over until the screams died in her throat and her eyes fluttered open. Lifting her head, she blinked as she tried to focus on me.

"It's me, baby. It's just me. You're safe. You're okay."

"Enzo?" Her voice was raspy from screaming.

"You're here with me. I won't let anything happen to you," I promised her.

Her eyes skittered around the room and then came back to me. "I'm sorry," she whispered. "I was dreaming I was back there and..." She didn't finish what she was about to say, but she didn't have to.

"I know."

"Can I have some water?"

Her question took me off guard. "Yes. I'll get you some." It was only when I removed my hands from her shoulders and saw the white fingermarks on her skin that I realized how tightly I'd been holding her. A sharp pang of guilt shot through me. The last thing she needed was to be manhandled right now. "I'll be right back." Quickly, I slid off the bed and walked out to the living area and got her a bottle of water from the small refrigerator.

"Thank you," she said when I gave it to her.

I watched her take a long drink, then I sat down on the side of the bed. "Better?"

She stared down at the bottle in her hands. "No," she told me. "Are you?"

"Me?"

She nodded.

"I'm fine. I'm just concerned about you."

"Why?"

"Why?" I couldn't keep the incredulousness out of my tone.

"Yeah." She paused for a moment, and then the rest of the words came out in a rush. "Why, Enzo? Why are so concerned about a girl you barely know? Why did you risk your life to help me?"

Her eyes bore into mine, searching for the truth. And I gave it to her. "Because we made a deal, and I always uphold my end of a deal." *And because, deal or no deal, you're mine.* The truth of it slammed into me so hard it nearly sent me reeling backward on the bed. And in its wake, a flood of anxiety followed. But I fought it back. She wasn't my wife. She wasn't Alessandra. I could keep her safe. From the family. From her father.

From me.

"What if I want out of our agreement?"

Although the question was asked with an innocent curiosity, pain flared in the center of my chest. "Is that true?"

She hesitated, lowering her eyes as she frowned down at her lap, and the pain was replaced by hope. "Honestly, I don't know anything right now."

I wanted to touch her. To erase the memories of the other men. Men who'd taken what was mine. But I was afraid if I did, she would freak out on me again. I could see the tension in her body. The way she held herself so rigidly, so straight and tall. And yet I felt like the touch of a feather would shatter her into a million pieces.

My anger returned, unreasonable and violent, rushing through my veins. "We have an agreement, you and I. And I expect you to live up to your end of it." I stopped, closed my eyes, and took a breath before opening them again. "Not right now. Not tonight. But soon. We made a deal, Sera," I repeated. Even as I heard the words leave my mouth, I felt like the biggest *mezzo di merda*—piece of shit—in the world. But I couldn't stop myself from making these demands of her. I couldn't let her leave my life. Not now. Not yet.

She stared at me through tear-filled eyes and didn't say a word.

"Do you want to go back to your father? Because I can make that happen. I can pick up the phone right fucking now, and his men will be here to haul your ass back to Dallas in a matter of hours. Is that what you want?" I pressed.

"No," she whispered.

God, I was a fucking monster. Because the only thing I wanted to do right now was to push her back on the bed and shove my cock so far inside of her that there would be nothing and no one but me for her. No memories. No threat of her father. No mafia. Nothing. Just me and her until she gave in to me. "Sera."

Raw need colored my voice when I said her name. Hearing it, she inhaled sharply, and her eyes shot to mine. I wanted to tell her how I'd died inside when I found out she went missing. How the only thing that kept me from going completely mad was the fact that we had the video and knew who'd taken her. I wished I'd kept his heart, so I could present it to her now as a bloody offering to prove my loyalty.

But I didn't say any of that. I couldn't. The words stuck in my throat. Yet whatever she saw in my eyes, the pain and anguish and madness, it drew her to me like I was a white-hot flame. She leaned toward me until I reached up and cupped her face in my hand. "Sera," I whispered.

The touch of her lips on mine was something I never thought I would feel again as I'd waited for the call from Rene, telling me that he couldn't find her. Or that if he *had* found something, it was her dead body. The fear that I refused to let myself feel then rose inside of me now, making me desperate to feel her, warm and alive, beneath me. To smell her scent. To hear her voice call my name. To feel the pain of her nails digging into my skin, and the wet heat of her cunt wrapped around my cock.

"Sera." I moaned her name against her lips. A plea to let me bring her pleasure. Not pain. Not again. Never again. "I want to touch you." Softly, I bit her lower lip.

I felt her stiffen and pull away slightly, but I still had my hand cupped around her cheek and I brought up my other hand so she couldn't run away. Her eyes were wide as they locked onto mine.

"I won't hurt you," I told her. "I swear I won't hurt you. I only want to make you feel good. Please, allow me to do that for you. Let me do this for you. Let me show you how good I can make you feel."

"You've already done that. Before."

A fresh wave of guilt tore through me when I remembered how violently I'd taken her innocence. And even after it had happened, after I'd seen her tears and felt her pain, I couldn't keep my hands off of her and I'd taken her again in the bathtub. I'd tried to make it better for her that time, but I know it had to still hurt. And the men who'd had her in that fucking house—my gut clenched until I wanted to vomit just thinking about it— they hadn't given two shits about the woman they were using.

I pressed my forehead to hers, my hands gentle on her face even as my muscles shook with the effort it took me to hold myself still. "No," I told her. "I didn't. I was too rough. And I hurt you. And for that, Sera, I'm so sorry."

"You didn't know," she whispered.

I pulled away just enough that I could see her face. "I need to touch you." But I made no move to do so, knowing instinctively that if I forced her now, I would never get her back. Physically, I could take her body and do what I wanted with it. But that would make me no better than them. No, I couldn't take her the way I wanted to until I had her complete surrender. And that would take time and trust. So, for now, I needed to wait for her permission. Even if it fucking killed me.

My heart stopped as her eyes dropped down to my chest and her hand rose, slow and shaky, to touch me. I held my breath as I waited, so attuned to her I felt the heat of her fingers just before they brushed my bare skin. With a touch that was barely a touch, her fingertips skimmed over my flesh, tracing the circle of the tattoo that covered my pec.

My eyes closed, and I ground my teeth together as my body reacted to her touch, hardening to the point of pain. My breath sawed in and out of my lungs in short pants.

She pulled her hand away and turned her head, then swallowed hard. "I'm sorry, Enzo. I can't."

The monster inside of me rose up, growling his impatience. I wanted to reassure her and let her know it was okay. I understood it was going to take time. That some people dealt with trauma better than others. But I couldn't trust myself to speak. I wasn't used to being told no. From anyone. Leaving her alone on the bed, I headed for the whiskey. The only thing that was going to save her right now was if I got shitfaced drunk. And even then, it was questionable.

I threw back one glass and was pouring another when she followed me out to the other room. "What are you doing?"

"Getting drunk."

She didn't say anything, but I could feel her staring at me. I sighed. "Go back to bed, Sera."

Instead, she remained where she was. "Maybe I should stay somewhere else."

I swung around to find her standing just inside the room, twisting her hands nervously in front of her. "No. You'll stay here."

"Enzo..."

"I said you'll stay here. I can control myself, Sera." And I could. I would. Even if it fucking killed me. For her.

The look she gave me made it clear she didn't know whether or not to believe me. "I just thought it might be easier for you."

"For me? Or for you?" I took a long drink, wishing the alcohol would hurry the hell up and make me numb so I could escape these things I felt for her.

Her eyes dipped down to my sex and shot back up to my face. Her neck and cheeks flushed red. I was only wearing my boxer briefs, and my erection was obvious.

"Where would you go?" I asked her to get my mind off of her eyes on my cock.

She frowned and then shrugged. "I don't know. I could get a different room."

I fell back on the only thing I could. "That wasn't part of our deal, Sera."

Her mouth opened, and I fully expected her to tell me she wanted out. A request I would deny. But then she closed it again. Without another word, she went back into the bedroom.

"Jesus fucking Christ." I wasn't sure who I was cursing at. Sera, or myself. I poured myself another whiskey and chugged it down.

What the hell was this pull she had on me? I didn't understand it. And I didn't like it. But I was done trying to lie to myself about it. I barely knew her, and yet I was willing to risk my life for her. To kill for her. To deny myself...for HER.

I poured myself another whiskey. Walking over to the couch, I sat down with my drink and stared out at the lights of the city. I'd been obsessed with Alessandra when I'd first met her, too. It was my nature. But not like this. I'd been young then, with all of the randiness of youth. Hell, I had a hard on more often than not whether she was in the room with me or not. She was my first love, and what I'd had to do to her ate away at my insides for years. It still did. But she'd left me with no other choice. It was her or both of us.

And yet, sometimes I wondered what my life would be like now if I'd chosen her and somehow managed to live through it. Where would we be living? Would we have had more children? Would we be happy? Or would we have outgrown each other and I would've left the only family I'd ever known for nothing?

Alessandra would still be alive, but what would I be? *Who* would I be?

I couldn't imagine my life being anything but what it was now. Being a part of the mafia was all I'd ever known, and it wasn't as hard as people thought it was. There were rules we lived by. Clear, black and white rules. Rules that were never broken without consequences.

Sometimes this life was bloody and violent, but it was only that way to protect the ones we loved. To protect the rules that kept us alive and out of jail. My life was orderly. I knew my place as one of Luca's soldiers. And after Alessandra, I allowed myself to care for no one except him and Tristan. The two people who had been with me through everything, and who I could depend on to always be there because we protected each other and we followed the rules. If I had the need for a woman, I called Jade. I knew what to expect with her, and I liked it that way. There were no feelings involved. No uncontrollable hunger. She was pretty, and she knew how to conduct herself in whatever situation she found herself in.

She didn't fuck me up inside until I couldn't think straight. Until the fear of losing her twisted my guts into knots. No woman had ever done that. Not even my wife.

Until Sera knocked on my door and threw my world into a tailspin. I felt off balance. Distracted. And that wasn't good for me or the people I was sworn to protect. I should have Luca call her father and let him come and take her. I knew this. It would be the smart thing to do. The right thing to do. Because what would her life be with me? Would she end up six feet in the ground like Alessandra? Would she constantly try to run from me? She was trying to escape the world of the mafia, not become more entwined in it.

And if I forced her to stay, she would only grow to hate me.

With these thoughts swirling in my head, I inhaled deeply, and the scent of bleach burned my lungs. In the morning, I'd check her skin to make sure she hadn't done any serious damage to herself.

Getting up, I walked quietly into the bedroom. Sera was curled up under the comforter, but I knew by her breathing she wasn't asleep yet. Still, I was quiet as I crossed the room to where I'd left my clothes and retrieved the items she'd given me earlier. A ring, a watch, and a money clip. Then I got my cell phone.

I took them all back out to the sitting room with me and laid them out on the coffee table, studying them as I drank. I would find out who these things belonged to.

And I would kill them.

For her.

LOVE ALL ANIMALS

CHAPTER 7

Serafina

I woke slowly, bit by bit, rising up from the depths of my dreams only to be dragged under again, until finally I rose all the way to the surface of my consciousness and hovered there.

The first thing I became aware of were the smells. Mostly fresh linen from the soft pillow beneath my head and the thick comforter pulled up over my face. Once I lowered the blanket, there was the mouthwatering smell of bacon and coffee. It permeated the room until I threw off the covers and sat up, getting my bearings.

Enzo.

I heard him moving around in the other room and quickly got up to use the bathroom and brush my teeth. When I was finished, I splashed some water on my face and ran

Enzo's comb through my hair, wishing I had something I could use to pull it back off my face. I finally just tucked the sides behind my ears.

The bed was made when I emerged, and my suitcase was lying open on top of the comforter. The one I'd left in the trunk of my car. My shoulder bag was next to it, my cell phone lying on top.

The folded bag that contained all of the money I'd saved up was nowhere to be found.

Enzo's voice came from the doorway, and I looked up to find him leaning against the doorframe, his hair still wet from a shower I hadn't heard him take, wearing a pair of black, low-hanging sweatpants and nothing else, his arms crossed over his powerful chest and his expression carefully blank as he studied me. Except for his eyes. His eyes were as expressive as always. And right now, the way he was looking at me made me feel like prey.

"I had your car towed here from the club. Where is the charger for your phone?"

I had to think for a second. "Um, I might have forgotten it at Jade's. Did you go through my stuff?" I didn't ask how he'd gotten into my car without the keys. I could guess.

He ignored my question. "I'll have the concierge get you another charger. Are you hungry? I had breakfast brought up from the kitchen."

I was having trouble keeping up with my thoughts. Possibly an aftereffect from the drugs? "Yeah. Yes. I'm starving."

"Good." He sounded relieved, like food would solve everything. And actually, to us Italians, it kind of did.

But instead of going back out to the other room, he walked over to the bed and sat down. "Before we eat, come here, please."

I hesitated, but only for a second, before I walked over to him. It wasn't because I was afraid of him. It was just...I didn't know what it was. A reaction to waking up and not quite believing I was here. Reaching for my hand, he pulled me forward until I stood between his legs. In a complete swing of emotions, I had the sudden impulse to throw myself into his arms and hug him tight, but I restrained myself. Taking a deep breath, I forced myself to hold still.

"I just want to check your skin to make sure the irritation from the bleach is calming down."

I still didn't feel clean, but now that my head was clearer, I could probably resist the urge to shower in bleach again.

When he stared at me meaningfully, I held out my bare arms. The skin was still a little irritated, but not nearly as red as last night. "I think it's okay."

But, of course, he wouldn't be happy until he checked for himself. "Let me see."

I held out my arms again and he took each one, turning it this way and that as he checked for any serious damage. "How is your wrist?"

I tested it. "Sore, but better."

"Good. Where else did you wash?"

I could tell by his tone that arguing with him would be futile. Lifting my shirt, I showed him my stomach.

He looked at it, but didn't tell me I could lower my shirt. Instead, I watched as he slowly raised his hand and skimmed his fingertips along the waistband of my yoga pants, his touch soft on my irritated skin. "Still so beautiful," he murmured.

My heart skipped a beat, and when it resumed its pace, it started to race. I closed my eyes as I swayed toward him, my lips parting on a surprised breath that I could still feel excitement from his touch.

One of his hands covered mine where it held the bottom of my shirt, and he lifted it higher, exposing the bottoms of my breasts. Leaning in until he was barely an inch from my sensitive skin, his nostrils flared as he breathed me in before he withdrew.

I was surprised at the disappointment that struck me. But then my breath caught when I felt his touch wander over my ribcage and up, up to the full underside of my left breast.

Slowly, he lifted my shirt higher, until I was fully exposed to the cool air all the way up to my collarbone. My nipples puckered with the chill, and I saw and heard his sharp inhale. His fingertips slowly circled one, and then the other.

I felt drunk. My eyes, half closed, were on his mouth. I'd never seen such perfect lips on a man. Not too full. Not too thin. And I wished more than anything that he would lean forward again and take my nipple between his teeth. There was a heavy pull on my womb and a rush of moisture between my legs as I imagined what it would feel like. If I stepped forward just a bit, and he bent his head down, I could make it happen. But I just...I couldn't.

"Beautiful," he said again. He had no idea how badly I wanted him to touch me. And how completely terrified I was that he actually would.

I bit back my moan of disappointment when he carefully lowered my T-shirt. "Anywhere else?" he asked. His voice was husky with longing.

I shook my head, not trusting myself to speak.

He suddenly stood up from the bed, forcing me to take a step back. My eyes landed on his chest, all tatted skin and muscle, and I swallowed hard.

"Sera?"

My name was soft on his lips, part question and part plea, and my eyes rose to meet his. His were...hungry. It was the only way I could describe it. I held my ground for only a few seconds more and then I stepped back away from him. "Is the food still warm?"

I felt his eyes on my face, but I couldn't look at him. "It should be," he told me after a moment. "If not, I'll send it back to the kitchen and get more." Then he waited for me to precede him from the room.

I turned away from him, trying to understand what it was I was feeling. I could identify an attachment to Enzo now that hadn't been there before that asshole from the club threw me in his trunk. Was it just because he'd rescued me? Or because he was really the only person I had right now? The only other friend I had was Jade, and she thought I was long gone. And for her own safety, I wanted to keep it that way.

"I ordered a bit of everything," he said as I made a surprised sound when I saw how much he'd ordered. "I wasn't sure what you liked."

"Thank you," I told him. A multitude of trays were lined up just inside the sitting room. They'd even brought in a small, square table and two chairs and set it over by the window. A vase sat in the middle with two red roses, identically bloomed. A coffee cup and a glass sat at each setting.

I picked up my plate to serve myself, but Enzo took it from me with a shake of his head. "Sit down. I'll get it for you."

Still shook up from what had just happened in the bedroom, I sat down at the table. I left him the seat where his back would be against the wall, knowing he would just move me if he needed to so he could sit where he could view the entire room. Soldiers were like that. It was ingrained in them from a young age when they were groomed to become the killers they were.

"Coffee? Or juice?"

I blinked, startled from my thoughts. "Both, please. With cream and sugar."

"I have a doctor coming up to see you in about an hour," he informed me as he filled my plate.

I didn't like doctors. I'd seen too many of them in my life. My father would have the status of my virginity confirmed on a weekly basis. "Why? What kind of doctor?"

Setting the full plate of food down in front of me, he briefly met my eyes before he took my coffee cup to fill it. "I want to make sure you're physically okay, Sera." He brought my cup back, setting the cream and sugar on the table near me.

I felt my face heat as a wave of embarrassment swept through me and I ducked my head. If there was anything wrong with me now, I didn't want anyone to see it. The doctor would know what happened to me. He would know how I'd been used...

"Hey." Enzo lifted my face with a hand cupped around my jaw. "Don't do that. You have nothing to be ashamed of. None of this was your fault."

My eyes filled with tears, even though I knew he was right.

Seeing them, he dropped down to his haunches in front of me, pulling my chair around until I was facing him and taking my hands. "You can't let them win, baby girl," he told me, and although he spoke softly, there was an edge of steel in his deep voice. "Don't let them fucking win."

I sniffed back my tears and nodded. I always thought of myself as a strong person. I had to be, growing up with my father. But being sold into prostitution was not something I'd ever imagined myself dealing with.

"We'll have the doctor check you out, make sure there was no damage, especially since you were drugged and may not have been aware, or remember what was going on." He paused, his dark eyes consuming me as they searched my face. "Is there any chance you're pregnant?"

Even though I'd thought the same thing, the fact that *he* was asking caught me off guard. "I don't think so. I think I had my period right before you showed up. That's why he washed me." The only other explanation for the dried blood on my thighs was something I didn't want to think about.

Though he didn't move from where he was or tighten the hold on my hands, I sensed the way his entire body became rigid. "Who washed you?"

"The guy who ran the house. The one I told you about. He just"—I thought back to that last day, trying to see through the fog of my memories—"hosed me down outside."

Enzo looked at me like he couldn't believe what he was hearing. "He fucking hosed you down? Like a goddamn dog?"

I remembered the ice-cold water hitting my naked skin like a thousand needles. But still, "It was good to feel clean," I told him.

He clenched his jaw, clearly not liking what that implied. I glanced at him. He was angry. Because he cared for me? Or because he considered me his property and someone else had touched something he owned without his permission?

After a long moment, he brushed back my hair with his fingers and stood, the movement smooth and graceful. "We should eat before breakfast gets cold." Turning my chair back around, he pressed a kiss to my temple and went to get his own food. As he spooned eggs on his plate, he said casually, "If you need to talk to someone about what happened to you, Veda has a really good therapist that she likes. I'm sure she would make time for you."

I picked up my fork as he sat down across from me. My stomach growled as I looked down at the pile of food he'd given me. "Who is Veda?"

"My boss's woman. Luca."

Luca, the underboss. "Oh."

"Do you want me to make an appointment? You don't have to worry about the cost."

"No," I immediately told him. "Thank you, though," I added when I realized how short I sounded. I'd had enough of therapists to last me three lifetimes. And after the last one accused me of stealing things because I wanted my father's attention, I'd be perfectly happy never to see one again.

"Sera, it might help," he said.

I set my fork down. "How am I supposed to talk about something I don't even remember?" That wasn't true. Not completely. I did remember some of it. Times when I wasn't given my next dosage on time and the stupor began to wear off. Or when the pain forced its way through. But even so, what was there to say? It happened. And now it was over, thanks to the man sitting across the table from me. I just wanted to forget all of it and go on with my life.

"Maybe you can talk to me," he said. "If you want to."

I stared at him across the table. This hard man who was trying so hard to be patient with me. I could see the way he practically vibrated with the effort it took him.

"I want to know everything about you, Sera. The good and the bad."

His words jostled something inside of me. I looked down at my plate and cut off a bite of pancake with my fork, sticking it into my mouth.

"What?" he asked. "What's with the face?"

The syrup was sticky sweet on my tongue, but it was hard to enjoy it with him sitting there staring holes in me.

"Sera. Goddammit. Talk to me."

So much for that patience. I sighed and put down my fork. "I can't. I don't want to. I just want to forget it ever happened."

"It's not that easy, Sera."

"Why not? I just want everything to go back to normal. Why can't you just let it go?" My eyes burned with tears. I didn't want to think about what happened to me. I didn't want to talk about it. I just wanted to eat this food that tasted so fucking good to me and then I wanted to take another shower and maybe zone out on a stupid show on Netflix.

He sat back in his chair. "Because I should've stopped you from leaving. I should've found you sooner. I should've *protected* you, Sera. And I didn't."

"I'm a grown woman, Enzo. One who makes really bad decisions sometimes. And you won't always be there to protect me." We sat staring at each other across the table. He didn't like that answer. But it was true. "Besides—"

"Don't even fucking give me the 'we barely know each other' bullshit," he bit out.

"But it's true," I told him softly.

He shook his head, but he didn't say anything else. Lifting his chin toward my plate, he said, "Stop fighting with me and eat your breakfast. The doctor will be here soon."

Grateful to stop talking, I dug back into my pancakes. I felt like I hadn't eaten in...well...a week.

We'd just finished when there was a knock on the door.

"I'll get it." Enzo ran into the bedroom first, pulling on a black T-shirt as he walked over to the door.

The doctor Enzo had called was a short, portly woman who looked to be in her fifties with kind eyes and a business-like manner. She took me back into the bedroom and chased Enzo out when he tried to follow us, then closed the door in his face after telling him we'd be out shortly.

I almost smiled at the shocked look on Enzo's face right before he was shut out.

"Okay, let's take a look at you," the doctor said after I'd gone into the bathroom and changed into a gown. I'd gotten to thinking while we were waiting for him that it wouldn't be a bad thing to get an exam. Although I felt okay, Enzo was right. I could have some kind of internal damage. Or worse, I *could* be pregnant. The doctor indicated for me to lie on the edge of the bed where she'd covered the mattress with a sterile sheet. "I apologize for the lack of a professional setup. Just lie here like you normally would on an exam table and scoot down to the edge, leaving your heels on the bed. Enzo told me you've had a rough time this past week."

I handed her the clear plastic cup I'd just peed in. "You could say that," I told her as I got into position.

"I'll try to make this as quick as possible," she told me.

Sitting down on the chair she'd pulled up to the bed, she told me to relax my legs, and I did, letting my knees fall open. She had a bright light standing next to the bed. I wondered where it came from. "How often do you make house calls like this?" I asked her to take my mind off what she was doing.

"Oh, you'd be surprised," she said. "I've been working for the family for quite a few years now. I have an office, but I rarely use it. I don't mind, though. It gets me outside."

I stared at the ceiling and tried to relax.

"Do you remember having any pain, Sera?"

"Some cramping. I thought it was my period."

"And when did that start?"

"I don't remember exactly. It usually only lasts three days. Sometimes four. I'm on the pill, but I wasn't taking them this past week."

She made a knowing sound. "Were you due to get your menstrual cycle?"

I tried to think back. "Honestly, I don't remember. But they're in my bag. I could check."

"Okay. That's fine." She pulled her instrument out of me and pulled the gown back down over my knees.

I lowered my legs and sat up.

"I didn't see anything that won't heal up pretty quick," she told me in a sympathetic voice. "But if you have any pain or any other concerns, call me right away."

"Okay."

"I don't know everything that happened to you, but if you feel up to it, it's perfectly okay to have sex again. Or to wait. It's up to you and what you're comfortable with, Sera. But physically, you should be fine. And you can go ahead and start taking your pills again."

I nodded to let her know I understood. "Can I go get changed?"

She smiled. "Yes. I'm finished."

"Thank you," I told her. "For coming here and doing all of this."

"No need to thank me," she said. "Mr. Delligatti paid me very well to make a house call."

After I was dressed again, I joined her and Enzo out in the other room. The doctor was giving Enzo a full report, and she smiled again when she saw me. "The preliminary pregnancy and STD tests came up negative, but I'll send them to the lab just to be safe, so still take precautions until you hear from me."

I nodded, as a feeling of relief nearly overwhelmed me. "Thank you."

She handed me a card. "Call me anytime if you need anything."

Taking it from her, I thanked her again.

"Thank you, doctor," Enzo told her as they shook hands.

I watched Enzo as he walked the doctor out to the hall with mixed feelings. Now there was nothing to keep him from insisting I live up to my end of our deal.

Only thing was, while I was lying in there, I decided I wanted out.

CHAPTER 8

Enzo

Sera spent the day curled up on the couch with her legs tucked under her, watching television while I did what I could for Luca via my phone and my laptop. She'd showered after the doctor's visit as I'd hovered outside the door to make sure she didn't try to scrub off her skin again, and seemed happy to be in her own clothes, but otherwise she was rather quiet, and I let her be. After rifling through her suitcase that morning and seeing what she was wearing now—black, baggy cotton pants and a Ramones T-shirt—I found that Sera's style was a little bit punk and a little bit classic vintage. Old concert T-shirts, loose patterned pants and skirts, baggy jeans with strategically placed tears, belts, boots, platform sneakers, plaid dresses. Quite a difference from the seductive costume she wore at the club. And yet, much like her pink hair, I liked this look on her.

Finished with my work for now, I got up from the desk, glancing over at her as I joined her on the couch. She kept her eyes on the show she was watching, not looking at me even when I touched her foot. "How are you doing?"

She gave me a quick glance. "I'm good. Thanks."

"Are you hungry? Would you like me to order dinner?" She didn't answer me. "Sera?"

After a moment, she hit the mute button on the television and set the remote on the coffee table. "Enzo, where is my money?"

I didn't pretend not to know what she was talking about. I'd found a large wad of cash folded up inside of a canvas tote bag that was rolled up on top of her clothes. It wasn't a lot, but it was enough for her to support herself somewhere else for a month, maybe two, along with the pay she'd tried to collect from the club when she was taken. It was money she'd wanted to use to leave me. To run away. "I put it somewhere safe for you."

"I'd like it back."

"It's safe. You don't need it when you're with me."

"I still want it back."

"I told you it's safe."

Changing position, she turned to face me. Took a deep breath.

No.

I knew what was coming before she even started to speak.

"Enzo, I appreciate everything you've done for me. I really have."

No.

"But I'd like to ask you to release me from our agreement."

"No."

She must've expected my answer, for not one iota of surprise flickered across her face. "Enzo, please. I don't think this was a good idea."

"Sera, if this is about what happened to you, I'm not going to push you into anything physical. Not until you're ready." I paused. "I'm trying very hard to be patient."

"That's not it," she said. "I mean, that's not all of it."

"Then what?"

"It's just..." She looked away, gathering her thoughts before her beautiful eyes came back to me. I willed myself to be still. "This was a mistake."

"No, it isn't."

"Enzo, please. I just want out."

No.

"I want to leave. This was a bad idea, and I was stupid to take you up on it. And I apologize. I don't want your money. I don't want anything. I just want to leave. I don't feel safe here."

"You don't feel safe with me?"

"No."

An aching chasm opened in my chest as color rose in her face, and I knew exactly what she was talking about. "I didn't know you were a virgin, Sera. You can't blame me for that."

But she was shaking her head. "No. No, that's not it."

"Then what the hell is it?" I was growing impatient with this conversation.

She threw her hands up in the air. "Enzo, I know next to nothing about you except that you're one of Luca's soldiers, and your life is exactly what I'm trying to escape."

"What do you want to know?"

Her eyes softened. "Enzo, it's too late."

"WHAT do you want to know?"

She shook her head, the ends of her pink hair brushing her shoulders.

Leaning forward, I jabbed my hands into my hair. This wasn't fucking happening. Resting my elbows on my knees, I forced down my panic. "I'm sitting here, offering to tell you whatever the fuck you want to know about me. The least you can do is give me a fucking chance. So *tell me* what you want to know."

At first, I thought she wasn't going to answer. I glanced over at her. Her chest rose and fell with quick breaths. Her jaw was set stubbornly, but then our gazes clashed, and I saw a flash of uncertainty in her eyes. "Something," she finally said. "Anything!"

A flicker of hope sparked within me. "All you need to do is ask me, Sera."

She crossed her arms over her chest and gave me a hard stare. "Okay. Tell me. How many other arrangements like this one have you had with women? Or men, for that matter?"

That was easy. I stared back, hoping she would see the truth in my eyes. "I've never done this before."

That seemed to take her aback. "So, this isn't a thing with you? Taking women off the streets and offering them money to have sex with you?"

I smiled at the surprise in her tone. "No. This isn't *a thing* with me. I prefer the emotional distance of escorts. Plus, they're a lot less expensive. I only have to pay them for one night at a time."

"Then I don't understand why you're doing this now. With me."

"What is there to understand? I wanted you, Sera. And after you tried to run from me, this was the only way I could have you."

"You could've just asked me out to dinner. Like a normal guy."

But that would've given her more of a chance to turn me down. "I'm not normal. And neither is my life."

"So you've never loved anyone? Never been in a relationship?"

"I didn't say that." She waited for me to say more. I didn't want to. "It's not important."

But I'd piqued her interest. "I'd like to hear about it anyway."

I scrubbed my hand over my face, feeling the growth of stubble on my jaw. I didn't like talking about my wife and son. That was a different time. A different me. Well, maybe not so different. But I could tell by the look in her blue-gray eyes that she wasn't going to let this go. "I was married. Once. When I was young. And we had a son."

"Where are they now?"

"They're not here anymore."

I saw the way she tried to hide her surprise. "What happened to them?"

"They're dead," I said flatly, biting down on the pain that threatened to rise from the depths of my core, where I kept it shoved down in my own personal hell. "And it was my fault." I hadn't said that out loud since my wife's funeral, but I felt the heaviness of that statement weigh me down until I felt like it was crushing my lungs. It was the truth, and there was no escaping it.

Her hands flew up to cover her mouth. "Oh, my god. Enzo, I'm so—"

"Don't," I told her, cutting off what she was about to say.

"Don't what?"

"Don't look at me like that. Don't feel sorry for me."

She lowered her hands back down to her lap. There were tears in her eyes. For me? Or for the innocent woman and child I'd killed? Well, technically, I hadn't killed my son. But he was dead because of who I am. "What were their names?"

"Sera, I don't want to talk about this."

There was a flash of hurt in her eyes that she quickly tried to hide. Biting her lower lip, she looked away.

With a heavy sigh, I said, "My wife was Alessandra. And my son's name was Elliot. He was three when he was shot by a stray bullet that was meant for me. He died in my arms. My wife went crazy after that, and she died a few months later. And I don't ever want to talk about it again."

Sera stared at me, unmoving, her eyes wide and glassy with unshed tears. She didn't try again to tell me she was sorry, or any of the other things people say when they don't know what to say in the face of your grief. And for that I was grateful. It made me want to hit the person who was saying it. They couldn't possibly understand what I'd gone through. What I was still going through every fucking day.

Slowly, she rose from her end of the couch and walked over to me. I didn't realize how tightly wound I was until she tried to move me. Taking my hand, she pulled my arm away from my body and sat down sideways across my lap, forcing me to sit up and make room for her. Her flowery coconut scent washed over me, and I closed my eyes and breathed her in, feeling some of the tightness leave my chest. I realized then that I didn't remember what Alessandra had smelled like. Or the way she'd felt in my arms.

My heart began to pound, and I suddenly went cold. How could I not remember my own wife?

Sera wrapped her arms around my neck and leaned against me, pressing the softness of her curves against my chest and tucking her face between my neck and my shoulder. She didn't say anything. She just held me.

Gradually, I felt the stiffness leave my muscles, and I leaned back against the couch cushion, taking her along with me and pulling her tight against my body. I found the pain was bearable so long as she held me together, and I was afraid that if she let go, the guilt and rage would burst from me, and I didn't know what I would do.

We sat for a long time as I silently battled my demons. She didn't ask me anything else, only offering her touch to help me get through it.

If only she knew that the man she was trying to comfort was the one who had pulled the trigger.

My bloodied hands wandered up and down her back, and when she didn't protest, I slid them beneath the hem of her shirt until I felt her warm, smooth skin. I had no right to touch her. She was still so innocent. Without sin. And I was a monster. But I needed this. I needed her.

I moaned when I realized she wore nothing underneath, my blood rushing to my cock until it swelled against her hip. "Sera." I skimmed my mouth along the side of her throat. "Stay with me." Her pulse fluttered against my lips as she took a shaky breath. "Stay with me, and let me show you how good we could be together. Let me make you happy."

She pulled away until she could look at me. "How would you do that when you represent the exact thing I'm trying to escape?"

I did. But I wasn't her father. My prison would be much more pleasurable. "Just give me a chance," I told her. "That's all I'm asking."

Her eyes wandered over my face. When they stopped on my mouth and the tip of her tongue shot out to wet her lips, my heart began to pound.

Carefully, I leaned in and brushed my mouth over hers. It was barely a touch at all, but I heard her breath catch and felt her start in my arms, like she'd been hit with the same jolt of electricity I had. I didn't retreat, but I also didn't push her. If I scared her away now, I didn't know that I'd ever get her back. So I did nothing else but gently taste her sweet lips with my lips and tongue, teasing her until she began to respond.

She kissed me back with tentative brushes of her lips, gradually allowing me more and more access to her mouth as my hands began to rub her back, soothing her even as my blood began to burn. I couldn't hold back my moan when I felt her tongue begin to tentatively explore my mouth. She tasted sweet. Like the honey in the tea she'd drank after lunch. I wanted to toss her onto her back and rip her pants off and throw her legs over my shoulders, but I pushed the thought out of my head, allowing her to set the pace.

When she broke off the kiss, I pressed my lips along her jaw, making my way over to the delicate lobe of her ear. She shuddered, goosebumps running down her spine beneath my hands when I sucked it into my mouth and played with the diamond stud with my tongue. "Let me show you, baby," I whispered into her ear.

Her head fell back as I made my way down her throat. When I reached the sensitive spot between her neck and shoulder, she rolled her hips, rubbing her ass along the hard length of my sex, her body knowing instinctively what to do despite her lack of experience.

I growled deep in my throat and sank my teeth into the muscle, just hard enough to hurt a little. I was burning alive, dying to be inside of her, and I stood, taking her with me, the only thought in my head to get her in the bedroom before I caught myself. I froze and searched her face, looking for any sign of fear. "Let me take you to bed. I swear I won't do anything you don't want me to. At any time at all, if you want me to stop, I'll stop." Blood pulsed through me with every hard beat of my heart as I waited for her answer. "Let me help you forget, Sera."

After a long time, she nodded. "Okay. But—"

I shook my head. "You don't have to say anything. If you want to stop, we stop."

Her eyes searched my face. Then she leaned in to kiss me again, wrapping her arms tight around my neck.

I wasted no more time getting her into the bedroom, breaking off the kiss as I climbed onto the mattress and laid her out beneath me. "Are you hurt? Are you hurt anywhere?" The doctor only told me there was nothing wrong with her that wouldn't heal, but she didn't go into any details.

She shook her head. "I don't think so. The doctor said this was okay if I felt up to it."

"I don't want to hurt you." Leaning over her, I brushed her pink hair from her face and spread the soft strands out on my pillow. "You have to tell me if I hurt you. Promise me."

"I promise," she whispered.

Reaching over my head with one hand, I pulled off my shirt and threw it on the floor, then settled myself on top of her. Her thighs opened to make room for me, and her hands fell to my shoulders as I began to kiss my way down her throat, reaching for the bottom of her shirt and lifting it until the smooth skin of her stomach was exposed. I ran my tongue along her ribs to the underside of her breasts. Slowly, like I was unwrapping a precious gift, I lifted her shirt higher, much as I had earlier, until her dark mauve nipples were exposed, following every inch of skin I revealed with my mouth. "Take this off," I ordered.

Sera lifted her upper body until I could pull her shirt off and toss it onto the floor with my own. Then, with a quick glance at her face to make sure she wasn't freaking out, I added her pants to the pile.

When I had her naked and spread out before me, her expression clouded and she didn't seem to know where to look, her hands automatically moving to try to cover herself. Gently, I took them within my own. Her skin was still red where she'd scrubbed it with cleanser. And she was still a little thin. But to me, she was perfection. "So fucking beautiful," I murmured. "Sera..." Her name was said on a reverent breath. "...you're so goddamn fucking beautiful."

Her eyes locked onto my face and unlike her, I didn't look away. "You stun me with your beauty," I told her. "You take my fucking breath away."

Her lips parted at my words, her arms relaxing her sides.

Releasing one of her hands, I pressed my palm flat to her belly, just above the soft curls between her thighs. Taking my time, I slid it up between her breasts until I could feel her racing heart. "There were times, this past week, when I wondered if I'd ever be able to touch you like this again," I admitted.

"I did too," she whispered.

I raised my eyes from her breasts until they clashed with her gaze. "It fucking terrified me." Our eyes connected as an unspoken communication passed between us.

Lowering my hips between her legs, I took one hard nipple between my teeth, rolling it around on my tongue until she moaned and squirmed beneath me. Then I released it and did the same with the other side before kissing my way down her stomach. I needed the taste of her on my tongue.

"Enzo..."

Her voice was shaky. Unsure.

Not now. Fucking hell, baby. Don't tell me to stop now.

Draping her legs over my shoulders, I ran my tongue between her wet folds until I found the sweet spot that made her hips buck.

"Enzo!"

CHAPTER 9

Enzo

"Oh, god..."

Sera's cries of passion were something I wondered if I would ever hear again. Her thighs clamped down on my shoulders, and I laid my arms over her hips to hold her still as her orgasm crashed over her. Before she had a chance to come down, I climbed over her, shoving my pants and boxer briefs down as I went until my cock sprang free. Come leaked from the head and I gripped myself in my fist, spreading it over her as I probed at her entrance.

"Enzo. Stop. Please. Stop. STOP."

I barely heard her pleas through the haze of lust and the pounding of my pulse in my ears. Grinding my teeth until my jaw hurt, I froze above her. "Sera," I breathed. I wasn't above begging at this point. I needed to be inside of her. To feel her around me, warm and alive and screaming my name.

But she was stiff with fear beneath me. And her eyes, when they met mine, were bright and wild. "I'm sorry... I'm s-sorry." Her voice was thick with tears.

They banked the fire inside of me enough so that I could hear her. I held myself completely still above her, my arms shaking with the effort. Looking down, I saw her eyes were squeezed shut and her face was a mask of fear. "Hey, hey. Sera. Open your eyes, baby. Open your eyes and look at me."

She blinked her eyes open, gradually focusing on me.

"It's just me, baby girl. You're okay. It's just me."

Her eyes were red with tears. "I'm so sorry," she told me.

I pressed my lips to the corners of her eyes, tasting the salt of her fear and pain. "You don't need to apologize," I told her. "But you need to tell me what you need from me. Do you really want me to stop?"

"I don't know," she whispered.

"Did I do something wrong?"

"No." I felt her fingers dig into my shoulders and my painfully swollen cock jerked in response. I was still poised at her entrance, my entire body trembling with the effort it took to hold myself still. "I'm sorry," she said again. "It's just me. I'm just..." She looked around the room, her eyes a little wild. "...I was fine, and then...I wasn't." A sob caught in her throat.

She wasn't fine when I laid on top of her and was about to fuck her. "Okay," I told her. I rolled over, taking her with me until she was straddling my hips, her hands on either side of my head.

"What are you doing?"

"I'm giving you all the control, baby." My hands tightened on her hips. She adjusted her position, and I groaned as the tips of her breasts brushed my chest.

She stared down at me.

"You can get up any time you want," I told her. "Nothing is holding you down on this bed. Not even me."

She looked down at our bodies, so close to being joined. "Enzo, I'm..." A sob caught in her throat. "I'm dirty," she whispered.

Dirty? "What are you talking about?"

"I'm disgusting."

I stared up at her in disbelief, my heart pounding, watching as her face crumbled and tears dripped onto my chest. "Sera—"

"You don't know what they did to me, those men." Beautiful, lost eyes rose to meet mine. "All of those men. So many I couldn't keep track of them. At first, I couldn't remember. But now...now bits and pieces are coming back to me. They...hurt me. And I did nothing to stop them. I *couldn't* stop them..."

The bastards. The goddamn *fucking* bastards.

She was swiftly falling back into the hell of her memories. I could see it in the haunted look in her eyes and the way she was starting to try to draw in on herself so she could hide within her shame.

I couldn't allow her to do that. What happened to her was not her fault. And she didn't have one damn thing to be ashamed of. "Sera. Baby, listen to me. Are you listening to me?"

After a moment, she raised her head and looked at me with bloodshot red eyes.

"You are not any of those fucking things. You are not a victim. Do you understand? Bad shit happened to you. It happens to all of us. You can't change it. But you can choose whether or not these things will define you, or if you will leave them in the past where they belong.

And those men that hurt you? I wish I could kill every single one of them."

A glimmer of what I could only describe as hope shone from her eyes.

"I would happily peel the skin from their bodies and twist their cocks off with my bare hands. Then I would shove it down their throats until they fucking choked on it." The need for revenge pulsed through my blood, feeding the lust that already resided there. I raised my hips, sliding my hardened sex through her slick folds. "I'll do all of that and more to the ones I can find. I'll even let you help if you wish. Would you like that?"

Her answer was immediate as her eyes hardened. "Yes."

I smiled up at her. My sweet girl. "Are you going to let them win, Sera? All of those cock-less bastards?"

She shook her head, sending soft waves of pink hair sliding over her bare shoulders. "No," she gritted out.

"No," I repeated. "No one fucks you anymore without your permission. You choose who you're going to fuck. Only you."

Again, she looked down our bodies. "I want to fuck you," she said softly. "But I don't know what to do."

"Yes, you do. And I'll help you." I raised my hips slightly, sliding my cock along her core, and her breath caught, her nails clawing into the front of my shoulders.

"Oh, my god."

Grinding my teeth, I pushed my head back into the mattress. It took everything I had in me not to flip her over and force my cock as deep as it would go, but I wouldn't do that to her again. I needed to allow her to take this at her speed, because the way she was looking at me right now...she wanted me, but she was afraid. And it tore me apart inside. "Lift up a little."

I showed her with my hands what I meant, and she did as I asked. With one hand, I positioned myself at her entrance and pulled her down just far enough for me to sink inside of her a bit. "Do you feel me?"

"Yes," she breathed.

"Is that okay?"

"Yes."

I closed my eyes and took a few deep breaths before opening them again. "Let me in, baby. Just sit down on me."

She lowered her hips, and I slid another inch inside of her. I groaned when she stopped, and her eyes flew to mine. Her expression was a little bit panicked. "Is it hurting you?" I asked her.

She shook her head. "No."

I nodded. "Good. You're doing so good. Keep going, baby girl."

She took me a little bit deeper, and I had to let go of her hips and grip the comforter. "Ah! God...You're so fucking tight. You feel so good..."

I continued to tell her how fucking good she felt wrapped around my cock as she carefully took me all the way in. When she was fully seated on my hips, she stilled, her head hanging forward and all of that gorgeous pink hair hiding her face from me.

But I felt the way she shuddered, and I heard the catch in her chest. "Sera? Baby, look at me. Look at me," I told her, reaching both hands for her face and lifting her head.

Her eyes were squeezed shut, and her mouth was in a tight line.

Shit. I was losing her. "Serafina, eyes on me," I ordered in a hard voice.

She responded to my tone, opening them and finding my face.

"You don't think about that," I told her. "You don't think about them. There's no one here but me and you. Understand?"

After a few seconds, she nodded.

"It's just me and you, baby girl. Just us. Eyes on me," I said when she started to look away. "Right here." I pointed at my own eyes with two fingers. "You don't look away, you got it? You keep your eyes on me."

"Okay," she whispered.

"Okay," I said. Lifting her hands from the death grip she had on my chest, I laced my fingers through hers and pushed until she was sitting up straight. Fuck, I was so deep inside of her, and she was so gorgeous sitting on me like that. "If anything hurts, you tell me."

She nodded.

Bending my knees, I pushed up with my hips, talking to her to keep her focus on what was happening here and now. Her eyes never strayed from mine as she began to move above me, lifting herself up and down with timid movements at first, gradually gaining more confidence.

And then, as she stared down at me, her expression began to change.

Her eyes hardened and her upper lip curled into an expression of hatred. I could feel the change in her entire body, and I watched the transition with something akin to fascination. But I knew it wasn't aimed at me. Not personally.

Or hell, maybe it was. Honestly, right now? I didn't give a shit.

She released my hands and gripped my wrists, slamming them down onto the bed on either side of my head. She started moving faster. Harder. Fucking me until I clenched my teeth together with the effort not to come. And the entire time, she kept her eyes right on mine.

Sera was taking back her control.

I didn't enjoy being held down, and I could've reversed our positions quite easily. But I allowed her to do it, knowing that she needed this more than anything I could say to her or how good I could make her feel.

Shoving herself upright, she threw her head back and took her pleasure from me, one hand on her breast and the other going between her legs where her long, slender fingers found her clit. I watched as she played with herself, using me like I was nothing better than a damn vibrator.

And it was one of the most erotic fucking things I'd ever seen.

Not because a woman hadn't done this in front of me before, but because it was Sera. My innocent Sera. My hands found her hips, her breasts, her thighs. I needed to touch her everywhere.

Her breaths came fast and hard as she rode me, my pulse pounding in my ears and my cock swollen to the point of pain as I met her stroke for stroke. Angry sounds escaped her throat. Her hand left her breast, and she leaned back, reaching behind her to dig her nails into my thigh. I was so fucking deep inside of her. I'd never felt anything so fucking good. "Fuck me, baby girl. Yes. Ah! Fuck. Just like that."

I don't know if she heard me or if she was so lost in her own head, nothing would break through. But a few second later, her fingers started moving faster on her clit and her hips rocked almost violently over mine right before she stiffened and cried out, throwing herself forward over me as her cunt pulsed around my cock.

"Sera!" My orgasm ripped through me so hard I cried out and dug my fingers into her soft flesh as my body jerked and curled in on itself. I hugged her to me as I came, my face buried in the crook of her neck to smother my own cries of release.

We lay like that for a long time, just trying to breathe as I rubbed my hands up and down her back, over her hips and ass and thighs and back again. "Are you okay?" I asked her when I could manage to speak.

And she burst into tears. Hard, heavy sobs that splayed my chest open and tore out my heart.

I didn't try to stop her. She needed to get this shit out. And if she needed to take it out on me, I was perfectly okay with that. So I let her cry, letting her know I was there with my touch, until her sobs turned to a shuddering sigh and sniffles. "I'm sorry," she told me, her voice still thick with tears.

"Shhh...you're alright. I've got you."

"I don't know what the hell that was," she admitted.

"It was you working through the stuff you've been through."

"I'm not angry at you."

"I know that, baby."

"I shouldn't have—"

Tangling my hand in her hair, I tugged her head back until she was looking up at me with confusion. "Stop fucking apologizing," I told her. "You need someone to hit? You hit me. You need someone to curse and scream at? You scream at me. You need someone to fuck? You fuck me. I'm a big boy, Sera. I can take it." And I understood. "You do what you need to do, baby girl. But what I won't allow you to do is shut me out. I won't let you run away."

"You make it sound like you're not giving me the choice."

I met her stare. "Maybe I'm not."

After a moment, she snuggled into me and I could hear the uncertainty in her voice when she said, "I wouldn't know where to go right now anyway."

For the first time since I'd met her, I felt the tension completely leave my body, like I was able to breathe again. With her.

The day after tomorrow, we would have to go to Luca's. And that's when the real battle to keep her would begin. But it was a battle I was going to win.

Never again would I be forced to choose between my family and a woman I couldn't give up.

LOVE ALL ANIMAL

CHAPTER 10

Serafina

After two full days of hanging out in Enzo's hotel room, it was time for us to leave, and I was surprised to find I didn't really want to go. I was getting comfortable here, and I could be myself with just Enzo around as I tried to adjust back to a normal life. He never made me feel like a victim or a freak. He held me when I woke up from a nightmare that paralyzed me with fear. He talked to me when I needed to be distracted. And he left me alone when I just wanted to zone out and watch some stupid crap on television and worry about someone else's problems for a while.

The one thing he didn't let me do was be without him.

Little by little, I was learning to deal with the things that happened to me. But I still had a long way to go. And sometimes I wondered if this freaked out woman with the roller coaster emotions was just who I was now.

But the thing that really got me? He left things lying around the room for me to steal when my anxiety got the best of me.

At first, I didn't realize what he was doing. I thought he just decided not to put his watch on one day and left it on the nightstand. Or that he'd emptied his pockets in the bathroom, leaving money on the counter, and forgotten to put it in his wallet.

But the more I watched him, the more I began to understand that Enzo didn't do anything carelessly. Everything in this hotel suite was neat and orderly. Nothing went without his notice. So it was safe to conclude that he knew exactly what it was doing by leaving this stuff lying around. And he never said anything when I returned the missing items to where I'd found them. He'd just pick the watch up and put it back on his wrist.

I asked him again about my money, and this time he showed me a safe where he'd locked it away, opening it so I could see the tote bag. Pulling it out, I peeked inside, relief flooding through me when I saw the money I'd worked so hard to save up. Enzo waited patiently until I placed it back inside the safe, and then he locked the door and straightened, leveling those intense brown eyes on me. "I have no need of your money, Sera."

"I know that," I told him. "That's not what I was worried about."

He cocked his head and waited for me to explain.

Fine. He wanted honesty? I'd give him honesty. "I wouldn't put it past you to take it from me so I wouldn't be able to leave."

"And you'd be right. That's exactly why I took it," he told me without an ounce of shame. "But I don't plan to keep it. You can have it back when the time comes."

"And when will that be?" I asked him.

"I can't tell you that. We'll just have to wait and find out."

I was learning pretty quick that Enzo was nothing if not straight up with me. He didn't beat around the bush. And he didn't throw a bunch of pretty words at me. So I believed him when he told me that I would get my savings back *when the time came*. It wasn't what I wanted, but it was the best I was gonna get. And I was going to have to learn to live with it or leave without a dime to my name.

"Are you ready?"

I took one last look around the bedroom, checking that I hadn't forgotten anything. Although, I'd be surprised if I had since I'd never unpacked, and just put anything I'd worn right back into my suitcase in the dirty clothes section. "Yup."

Back in his work clothes, Enzo was quiet on the drive to Luca's, which wasn't unusual for him, but I could sense tension in the air that wasn't usually there, and it didn't do anything for my nerves. I was about to meet the notorious underboss who ran this city with a sharp blade and a no second chances attitude. Rumor had it he was about to usurp his father out of his position and take over as boss. I'd heard my father and his cronies talking about it before I came here. I'd also heard them say that Luca's main competition, his brother Mario, had mysteriously disappeared over the summer.

I turned from the scenery passing by my window as we headed out of the city and toward the lakes. "So, what's he like?"

Sunglasses in place, Enzo never took his eyes from the road except to check the mirrors every once in a while. "Who? Luca?"

"Yes."

"He's an underboss, Sera," he told me, as though no other explanation was necessary. "But he's also someone I've known nearly my entire life. You have nothing to be scared of."

"Nothing?"

He knew what I meant, and he didn't respond.

"Tell me again why I have to go here."

"Because it's where I need to be, and you'll be safer here. With me."

"But I thought you said you killed the asshole who shoved me in his trunk."

"I did."

"Then who am I hiding from? My father doesn't know I'm here."

"I told you, Luigi knows. Luca told him before he knew about us."

"But he hasn't told my father yet, right?" I knew I was acting like a child, but I couldn't stop myself.

He glanced over at me, then took my hand as he returned his eyes to the road. "I don't know what Luigi has done by now. But if he did, you'll be safe at Luca's. His home is off the main road and surrounded by guards. No one can get in or out without him knowing about it. Not even your father's men. It'll be okay." I felt his eyes on me. "Hey. Look at me."

I'd been twisting my hands in my lap nervously, staring straight ahead out the windshield without really seeing anything as he talked. I had the nearly uncontrollable urge to leap from the vehicle and run. But at his command, I took a steadying breath and turned to look at him.

"No one will take you anywhere you don't want to go."

I nodded, not trusting myself to speak around the bubble of fear rising in my throat.

Enzo reached over and grabbed my hand, lifting it to his mouth and kissing the back. He didn't let it go the rest of the drive.

A few minutes later, we arrived at Luca's. Enzo had told me how even his own family didn't know the location of his home, and the fact that he didn't blindfold me told me more than words ever could.

Guards greeted us at the gate, opening it immediately when they saw it was Enzo. We drove down a long drive crowded by trees, but between breaks in the branches I could see men with guns patrolling the grounds. We drove on until we came upon the house, a great, sprawling, two-story stone home easily twice the size of my father's house. A large fountain surrounded by native Texas plants sat in the center of the circular drive, adding to the grandeur.

Enzo pulled the SUV up to the front of the house. Before we could even get out, the front door opened and a man with short dark hair, a closely trimmed mustache and beard, and dead brown eyes came out to greet us. I vaguely recognized him as the man who'd been with Enzo when he came to rescue me from the house in Mexico. At the time, I'd been too out of it to think much about him. But now I realized that I should've paid much more attention.

Because he scared the ever-living hell out of me.

"This is Tristan," Enzo told me as he helped me out of the vehicle. "Tris, this is Sera."

He didn't offer his hand, and I was grateful. "I remember," he told me. I gave him a timid smile. With a nod, he went to the back of the car and helped Enzo with our suitcases. "I'll get your stuff," he told him. "Luca is in the kitchen with Veda. They're waiting for you."

"Thanks," Enzo told him. Taking my hand, he led me into the house.

My eyes went wide as we walked into the foyer. It opened onto a great room with ceilings that reached all the way to the second floor, edged with crown molding. Straight ahead, a glass wall overlooked the lake. A small sitting area made up of a few comfy-looking chairs sat directly in front of it. Tiled stairs rose to the right with a beautiful wrought iron banister that extended along the loft-like walkway of the second floor that ran along the entire circumference of the room. Four great, rounded columns helped support it, giving the room a majestic feel.

On my left was a bar made of the same marble tiles as the floor, and just past it was another, larger, sitting area made up of a couch, a few more chairs, and a fireplace.

I was so enthralled that Enzo's voice startled me when he spoke. "There's a heated pool you can use year-round, a media room, and a gym downstairs. I'll show you around once we check in with Luca."

I realized my mouth was hanging open and slammed it shut. "This house is gorgeous."

He looked around as though he'd never noticed before. "Yes. It is. I normally stay here at night, monitoring the guards outside and the security cameras. It's part of my job."

I immediately felt a sense of loss that he wouldn't be lying beside me while I slept. "Oh."

"Along with my other duties," he added.

"When do you sleep?"

"Whenever I get the chance." He tugged on my hand. "Come. Let's go say hello to our hosts."

He led me to the other side of the room until we reached a couple of doorways. One led into a large kitchen made up of warm earth tones. A man and a woman sat at the table talking quietly, both with light hair—hers an ashy blonde and his darker and sprinkled with gray above his ears. His sharp blue eyes met mine the moment we appeared, and if Enzo hadn't been holding my hand, my automatic reaction would've been to take a few steps back.

This was Luca, the underboss. Even if we'd been in a crowded room, I would've known who he was. There was a sense of unmerciful power about him, tempered only by the possessive way he touched the woman with him.

When she saw his attention was diverted, she swung around, and her welcoming smile landed on me and Enzo. It didn't escape my notice the way her eyes warmed when they landed on the man standing beside me, and I felt a twinge of something cold and hard toward this woman.

It didn't last long, though, because it was difficult to have any kind of bad feelings toward someone who jumped out of their chair to rush over and give you a welcoming hug so hard you couldn't breathe.

"Sera, this is Veda," Enzo said. "Veda. Sera."

"I've heard very little about you," she told me once she'd released me from her death grip, "but I'm so happy to meet you."

"Thank you," I responded. "And I can say the same about you."

She laughed. It was a strange sound to me coming from a home like this. There was never laughter in my own growing up. Not so happy and carefree. "I like her already," she told Enzo.

Luca rose from the table and came to stand beside Veda. "It's nice to meet you, Sera. Please make yourself at home while you're staying here." He didn't offer me his hand either, and I was grateful, for mine were shaking.

"Thank you," I said. "I appreciate it."

His blue eyes roamed over my face, sizing me up, as he said, "Veda, why don't you show Sera where she'll be staying? I'll have a few of my men bring up your things."

"That's not necessary," I told him. "I only have a suitcase. And"—I waved in Enzo's direction—"so does Enzo."

"Please, allow one of the men to take care of it for you," he said. "I insist."

With no other choice, I gave him a nod. "Thank you."

He turned to Enzo. "Come to my office with me while Veda shows Sera around. I need to get you caught up on a few things."

Enzo squeezed my hand and released it. "I'll see you soon."

I gave him a small smile and followed Veda out of the room.

"Lisa, Luca's cook and general house servant, will be starting dinner soon. But if you're hungry or anything, we can scrounge you up something to hold you over after the tour."

"I'm good, but thank you." I frowned. "House servant?"

Veda nodded with a little laugh. "That's what I call her. She's the only one he'll allow to work here, so she cooks, buys groceries, cleans, and anything else he needs her to."

"Oh."

"Do you like to swim? The pool here is gorgeous..."

Veda rattled on as she gave me a tour of the floor we were on, then we headed upstairs. The house had six bedrooms, each with their own bathroom. She and Luca were in the largest room to the right. Enzo and I would be staying in the one farthest to the left to give us the most privacy.

"But if you need some alone time," she told me, "just do what I did and move yourself into another room. It confuses them and they don't know what to do about it." She grinned, but there was an edge of sadness to it. "Although I have to admit, the couple of times I did stay in my own room, it was because I wasn't in a good place. Luca let me have my privacy, but only until he decided that time was up."

"How do you do it?" I asked her quietly. I'd seen the security cameras throughout our tour, and I had no idea if there were listening ears attached to them.

"Do what? Oh, this is your room. What do you think?"

I looked around. The bedroom was decorated in shades of white. White walls, off-white carpet, white molding on the tray ceiling. The bed was also white, the color of the palest wheat, with a dusky blue comforter and pillows and a pale blue leather ottoman at the foot. But it was the wall of windows looking out over the lake on the far wall that drew me past the bed, underneath a dividing archway, and into the small sitting area directly in front of them. The loveseat and lounge chair matched the bed, creamy white with blue pillows. The sun was beginning to set, and the sky was red and pink and orange and blue over the water. It was beautiful.

"The bathroom is right through here." Veda pointed to a door to her left near the bed. "There's a full walk-in closet in there too."

"This is gorgeous," I told her honestly.

She joined me by the windows and plopped down on the lounge chair as one of Luca's men carried our luggage in and placed them near the bed. "So, what was your question?"

I dragged my eyes away from the window. "I asked how you do it. How do you live here with him? With Luca," I whispered. "Knowing what he is." Enzo had mentioned to me that Veda wasn't from our world, though he didn't go into detail about how she'd gotten here.

She glanced out the window as she thought about her answer. "It's not easy," she told me in a solemn voice. "But I love him, and he's not going to change. So it was either accept him for the man he is or live without him. I chose to be with him." She paused and her eyes became haunted with memories I wasn't sure I ever wanted to know. "Luca fought so hard for me. And we're both paying the price. But we have each other."

"Doesn't it scare you? I mean, he could get arrested. Or killed. And so could you just for being with him."

"It terrifies me," she admitted. "Luca is a powerful man, but he's not invincible, no matter what he believes."

"Yet you still stay with him of your own free will."

"Sure. *Now*." She laughed. "But at the beginning, our relationship was much more one-sided. His side. Not mine. And the only reason we even met was because he thought he was kidnapping my twin sister." A dark shadow passed over her pretty face. "I got caught up in the game being played out by Luca and his brother, and sometimes I'm amazed I survived at all." She shrugged. "But here I am."

I should've been shocked, but I wasn't. Not at all.

"You don't seem surprised," she said.

"That's because I'm not. My father is mafia. I grew up in this shit."

"Well, I guess that's good. You should have a much easier time adjusting to living here than I did. Hell, I still go to therapy."

Her smile was back, and I didn't want to ruin the mood by telling her the truth of my situation. "Are you and Enzo close?" I asked instead. "You seemed happy to see him when we came in." I hadn't meant to ask that question, but my mouth seemed to have a mind of its own.

"Mmm," she made an indecisive movement with her head, "I don't know that 'close' is the right word. Enzo doesn't let anyone in very much. Except maybe Luca and Tristan. But they have a long history. However, when things were bad with me and Luca, he was probably the closest thing I had to a friend since I came here. He was the one who always had to watch me, and we got to know each other a little bit. And he was teaching me self-defense, so we spent a lot of time together."

"Oh." I definitely didn't like the idea of how up close and personal the two of them would have to be for that.

"He would also die for Luca, and he and Tristan both have taken bullets meant for him. So, how could I not love him?"

I didn't remember seeing any evidence of previous injuries. But then again, it's not like I'd ever given his body more than an admiring glance. I'd always been too shy about it. Unlike Enzo, who probably knew every stretch mark and freckle I had after only a few nights together.

"I consider him a friend, Sera. Nothing more."

I blinked, coming back to our conversation. "Oh. No. I believe you. And it's fine either way. I was just wondering. That's all." The lies flew from my mouth, and I didn't know who I was trying to convince more, Veda or myself.

I couldn't grow attached to him. There was no way in hell I was going to end up stuck here like Veda. I wanted to be free.

And Enzo Delligatti could never be free. His world would always be ruled by the family of organized crime. And if I chose to be with him, so would mine.

CHAPTER 11

Enzo

"I have to tell my father she's here, Enzo. I'm sorry." I shook my head. "You can't do that."

"I have to."

"Why?" I shouted before I could stop myself.

Luca sat calmly behind his desk, non-reactive to my outburst. Only his eyes followed me as I paced back and forth like a caged animal. "You knew the deal when you went to go get her. And I'm sorry. If you would've told me about her before Tristan found her, I could've—"

"What?" I broke in rudely. "Could've what, Luca?"

"I could've given you more time."

"So, this is my fault."

"I didn't say that."

"Then what the hell are you saying? I should've left her in fucking Mexico?"

"ENZO."

I stopped my pacing abruptly, took a breath, and turned to face my friend. The expression on his face told me he was done taking my shit. I bowed my head. "I apologize. I shouldn't take my shit out on you."

Rising from his desk, Luca came to stand in front of me. "I know you feel some sort of obligation for this girl..."

I laughed. *Obligation.* What I felt for Sera was far from any sort of obligation. It was a fucking obsession.

Luca's blue eyes narrowed in on me. "What's really going on with you, Enz? Talk to me."

But I couldn't. Because how was I supposed to explain to him the things I was feeling when I didn't even fucking know? How her eyes and voice haunted every one of my thoughts and my body craved her more than food or water. How I'd spent the last few days learning every single fucking inch of her. Jesus, I could still taste her on my tongue and yet my mouth watered for more. The needy sounds she made were a constant orchestra in my ears. Even now, I was half hard. I walked around in a constant state of arousal until I could have her again.

And more than that, I was learning who Sera was. Her wants. Her needs. Her dreams. The things that had happened to her in that house in Mexico weighed on her now, dimming some of her light, but it was still there beneath the surface. I would catch glimpses of it every once in a while, and it would lighten my own dark soul the way nothing else could.

I craved that light, even as I tried to block it. She was a distraction. A dangerous distraction. But one I couldn't bring myself to give up. I wasn't ready to let her go. And yet, I knew that I would have to.

Just not yet.

Luca studied me. "There is one other possible solution," he said, "that would allow you to keep her."

My eyes met his through my sunglasses, and I knew what he was going to say before he said it. I shook my head. "No."

But he voiced it anyway. "You could marry her. We could make her father an offer of an alliance."

"No."

"Enzo…"

"No, Luca. That option is not on the table."

But he wouldn't back down. "Take off your sunglasses." It was a direct order. One I couldn't disobey, even though I'd left them on specifically because I knew Luca would see too much.

He waited patiently, and, knowing he would rip them from my face if I didn't do as he said, I raised my hand and yanked them off of my face, keeping my eyes averted.

"Look at me, my friend."

He wasn't playing fair. Left with no other choice, I did as he directed.

His blue eyes clashed with mine. It only took a few moments for him to comprehend what he saw. "You care for her."

"I care about fucking her."

"No," he said. "It's more than that. Much more."

"She's been through a lot. Because of me. Because I offered her protection and then I didn't provide her that protection. I think she's earned a respite before she's shipped back to her crazy father. That's all."

"Don't lie to me, Enzo."

I clenched my teeth together until they hurt.

"I know you haven't known her very long, but as I know from my own experience, that doesn't always matter." He sighed, and laid a heavy hand on my shoulder. "Would it be the worse thing in the world to have a wife again?"

"Yes." It would. I refused to subject Sera to the same thing I'd put Alessandra through. "Our life is too dangerous. Especially right now, with you going after

Luigi's position in the family. We don't know who our friends are or who our enemies are."

"If you married her, we could coerce her father to be on my side. He would be family. He'd have no choice. And whether we like his methods or not, he's rising in power up in Dallas. He would be a good ally to have." He paused. "If you don't, and we send her back without her virginity intact, what do you think he will do to us when I go after my father? What do you think he will do to *her*?"

"That's exactly why you can't send her back."

He stared at me, and I could see the way he struggled to understand my thinking. "You'd rather start a war than marry the girl?"

"I don't see you running off to marry Veda."

"Veda is not in the same position as Sera. She's not a mafia princess. And, for your information, I would marry her tomorrow if she would fucking have me. Don't think I haven't tried to talk her into it."

That surprised me. "You proposed? And she refused?"

"She did," he said, momentarily allowing me to sidetrack the conversation. He crossed his arms over his chest, pulling his black Armani jacket tight across his shoulders. "She has her reasons, and I can't fault her for them. She's not from our world, and although I know she loves me, making it official on paper...well, she just needs a little more time to adjust."

"Sera wants to escape this world. Just like Alessandra."

His eyes snapped back to mine, and understanding dawned. "Sera is not Alessandra. If anything, she's better suited to live this life than either your first wife or Veda. She's grown up in it. She knows what the deal is."

"That's all true. And because of all that, she hates this life even more, Luca. She's here in Austin because she ran from her father. Ran the first chance she had. She was little more than a prisoner and had to stop here to try to earn some money so she can start over somewhere else."

"And yet you sucked her right back into it."

"Temporarily," I insisted, even as the truth clawed its way up my spine. "And I didn't know who she was when we met."

"What did you offer her?" he asked.

There was no sense in not telling him. He would find out eventually one way or the other. "Money. Enough to allow her to start a brand-new life. A new name. New identification. And anything else she would need."

One eyebrow went up. "All of that for a girl you just want to fuck a few times?"

I tried to play it off. "Us Italians are a passionate bunch who go after what we want. Whatever it takes. Right?"

His eyes narrowed at the reference to him kidnapping Veda. "This is true," he finally said.

Running his hand through his hair, he paced away from me as I waited patiently for him to tell me what he was going to do. I didn't have to wait long.

"I'm sorry, Enzo, but with the circumstances being what they are, if you're not willing to marry the girl, I don't know how else to get around letting my father know she's here. And she will eventually go back to her father."

I stared down at the floor, my mind racing. But he was right. There was nothing else we could offer to Ciro Cordaro that would be worth anything to him. Except...

"Wait."

Luca gave me his attention. "What?"

"You said Ciro has been causing problems in his town, yes?"

"That's my understanding from what my connections have told me."

"And you want to get him on your side, to keep our relationship strong."

He cocked his head. "What are you thinking?"

I held my hand out in front of me, asking for patience. "We could use his daughter for leverage. Hold her here as our prisoner. Use her to get him to do as we wish."

But Luca immediately shook his head. "That won't work."

"Why not?"

"Because to Ciro, his daughter is nothing but a piece of virgin property for him to sell to the highest bidder. He won't give anything for her. And if we threaten her safety, he'll assume her value has gone down. But he still might start something to save face. To prove how tough and strong he is. And I can't afford to be involved in a war right now. Not with everything else going on with my father and after how carefully we've made every move to get to where we are now."

Goddammit. He was right. I knew he was right.

"I'm sorry, Enzo, but we have no other choice than to let Luigi know she's here. But perhaps I can talk him into waiting a few days before he lets Ciro know."

My blood raged through my veins, even though I knew he was right. We had no other choice. At least, not one I was willing to do. "What will you tell him?"

"I don't know." He gave me a small smile. "I'll think of something." He paused. "I'll tell him I want to keep her here to question her about her father."

I gave him a nod, then walked over to the table in the corner and poured myself a full glass of whiskey, downing it in one swallow.

"You can still change your mind," he said quietly. Before I could respond, he held up his hand. "Just think about it. You have a little time."

CHAPTER 12

Serafina

I quickly discovered that I liked Veda. There was something truly special about her, and I could see why Luca was so in love with her. Of that, there was no doubt. Even in the short time I'd seen them together, I could see that she was his entire world.

It almost made me wish that I planned to stick around longer, and maybe for the first time in my life I'd know what it was like to have a real friend.

After assuring me there was nothing going on between her and Enzo, and me continuing to insist I wouldn't care if there was, Veda changed the subject and started talking about the classes she was taking at the community college, and I was grateful so I wouldn't have to continue to lie to someone I truly liked.

We were commiserating over professors who insisted on giving their students essay only questions on their tests when Enzo came in.

My eyes went to him immediately, drawn by something I couldn't put a name to. But I knew something was wrong.

"Veda, would you leave us, please?"

She gave me a smile as she rose. "I'll see you at dinner."

"Okay. Thanks for the tour, and for keeping me company."

Enzo glanced at her briefly and nodded with respect as she walked past, then closed the door behind her, turning the lock. The soft click was obscenely loud in the sudden silence of the room.

My heartbeat was loud in my ears as he took off his sunglasses and watch and tossed them on one of the nightstands. Then he turned and came straight at me, the question I was about to ask dying on my tongue when I met his eyes. Something was horribly, horribly wrong. "What happened?"

He gave no indication that he'd heard my question. When he reached me, he grabbed me up in his strong arms and wrapped one hand in my hair to tug my head back and bring my mouth up to his.

The kiss was nothing like any we'd shared before. I could practically taste the desperation. The sorrow. The rage and confusion. I tried to break away, to talk to him, but he tightened his grip on the back of my head, holding me prisoner as he ravaged my mouth.

I pressed my hands against his chest and tried to shove him away, but it was like trying to move a wall. He made a desperate sound low in his throat that made my heart ache, and so, finally, I gave in and wrapped my arms around his neck.

As soon as he felt my surrender, he lifted me off the ground and carried me over to the bed. Enzo broke the connection between us only long enough to undress us both, ignoring my questions when I tried again to get him to talk to me.

Once there were no more barriers between us, he laid me back, following me down as his lips once again met mine. I sucked in a breath as he entered me with one strong thrust. I expected it to hurt, but it didn't. Not at all. I felt my body stretch to accommodate him, but there was no pain. Only a fierce stab of pleasure as my back arched and my legs opened wide to give him more room.

I felt his big body shudder on top of mine. "So wet," he whispered against my mouth. "So sweet."

My fingernails dug into the backs of his shoulders as, with a moan, he slowly pulled out before slamming back into me. One arm worked its way beneath my hips to pull me even closer, his weight braced on his other elbow beside my head.

Tearing his mouth from mine, he buried his face into my neck and took me hard and fast, breathing hard, his heart pounding against mine as with each strong thrust he moved us across the mattress until I hit the headboard.

I had no time to get too much into my head. To be scared. All I could do was feel the same sense of urgency as he tightened his arm around me, arching my body completely up off the mattress. Tension gathered in my lower belly with every hard thrust, his pelvis hitting my clit faster and faster, his lips whispering things too quiet for me to understand against my skin.

Just as I was hovering on the precipice, a low growl rumbled against my throat and his teeth sank into the muscle between my neck and shoulder. The pain mixed with pleasure, throwing me over the edge in a violent release just as Enzo stiffened above me, squeezing the breath from my lungs as he cried out and pushed himself impossibly deeper inside of me.

But he wasn't done.

He was just getting started.

We stayed in bed for hours as he fucked me every which way, until my muscles felt so slack I had no idea how I was going to walk back downstairs for dinner. But it wasn't the orgasms or the way he dominated my body that left me so exhausted, it was the emotion that poured out of him. The need he sucked out of me. Not with words, but with every touch. Every kiss. Every time I would try to talk to him, he would start kissing me. Or he'd shove my legs apart and put his mouth on me until I couldn't form a comprehensive thought.

And his eyes...his eyes burned me from the inside out, delving into my soul and dragging me down into his personal hell with him. After that first time, he didn't hide from me anymore, ordering me to open my eyes. To look at him. To watch. Until it was too much. Until I was nearly sobbing with the intensity of it. Only then did he release me, moving his gaze down my body, scorching every inch until I was surprised to see my skin was still unmarred when I looked down at myself.

And when he'd finally exhausted himself and we were lying in a tangle of sweaty limbs on top of the comforter, I tilted my face up to his. "Enzo, tell me what's wrong."

The crazed light in his eyes had dimmed, but at my words, it flickered back to life as they met mine, and at first, I thought he still wasn't going to tell me. But then he brushed a strand of my hair from my forehead and said, "We only have a few days until your father will be coming to get you. If Luca can get us that much time when he talks to Luigi." He didn't look confident in his boss's abilities. "He said he would think of some reason to keep you here as long as we could."

My blood, rushing through me like lava just a few minutes before, froze in my veins. "No."

"Sera, we have no other choice but to tell him you're here."

I shoved him away from me, sitting up and turning my back to the gorgeous man sprawled across the bed as I scooted my way off the opposite side. "*You* have no choice. But I fucking do. And I'm not sitting around here waiting for him to come get me and lock me back inside of my room." Or worse. But I didn't voice that fear out loud.

Enzo sat up and tried to grab my wrist, but I pulled it out of his reach and slid off the mattress. "Sera. There's nowhere you can go."

A thought occurred to me, and I whirled to face him with my shirt held in front of me. "Is that why you brought me here? So I couldn't get away?"

His brows drew together. "What? No—"

"Bullshit." Panicked now, I yanked my shirt over my head, not bothering to search for my bra, and scanned the floor for my pants. Finding them lying beneath Enzo's suit jacket, I kicked it aside and started pulling them on.

Enzo was off the bed in a flash and came around to stand in front of me. He grabbed my arms, forcing me to give up on my pants. I left them hanging somewhere below my hips and stared around his left arm with a mutinous expression as he tried to get me to look at him.

When I refused, he finally said, "Do you really believe I would do something like that to you?"

"Yes," I answered without even thinking about it. "Of course, you would. Your loyalty isn't to me. It's to Luca. To your mafia family. I understand that. And honestly, I'm not even mad about it." That was a slight understatement, but I didn't want this to turn into some kind of lover's quarrel. I just wanted to leave. "Where's my money?"

He was quiet for a minute, then he released my arms and took a step back. I kept my eyes averted from his naked form as I finished pulling on my pants. "Where is it?" I asked again.

"It's safe."

"I want it back. Now."

He didn't move. Didn't answer me.

I started to shake. If he wouldn't give me my money, there was no way I'd be able to survive even if he did let me go. "Goddammit, Enzo. That money is mine. I'm not asking you for anything else. I just want my clothes and my money and my car so I can get the hell out of here." As soon as the words were out of my mouth, I remembered that my car was still back at his hotel. "No. Know what? I don't even care about the car. I'll call an Uber."

He stood still and silent until I braced myself for his anger and looked up at him.

But it wasn't anger I found in his expression, it was loss. Utter devastation. Just for a second before he schooled his features and shifted his gaze to the side. "You're not going anywhere," he told me softly. "Not yet." Walking around me, he headed to the bathroom, closing the door behind him. A few seconds later, I heard the shower come on.

I stood there beside the bed where I'd just given this man my fucking soul, and he thought he could just make decisions about my life and then walk away?

Oh, hell no.

Flinging the door open, I marched into the walk-in closet you had to go through before you got to the bathroom and started searching for a safe or anywhere he could be hiding my money. The closet was empty except for our two suitcases, so it didn't take me long to see there was nothing of the sort in there.

Laying Enzo's suitcase on the floor, I opened it and started tossing his clothes around haphazardly, looking for my tote bag. It wasn't in there, either. Sitting back on my heels, I tried to think. Maybe he left it back at the hotel. We didn't check out when we left, but then again, he could've done it online or something.

"What are you doing?"

Enzo stood in the doorway of the closet wearing nothing but a low-hanging towel and a carefully blank expression.

"I'm looking for my money, what the hell do you think I'm doing?"

"It's not here, Sera."

I closed my eyes and tried to breathe. Slowly, I got to my feet. "Then where the hell is it?"

Crossing his arms over his chest, he leveled a steady stare at me that was strangely devoid of feeling. "I told you, you'll get it back when it's time."

"And when will that time be, Enzo? Huh? When you hand it over to my fucking father? It's not his money."

"No. I wouldn't do that."

As we stood there staring each other down, all of the fight suddenly drained out of me, and I crumpled to the floor as a cold numbness crept through my bones and reality slapped me in the face. There was nothing I could do. I was going back to my father. Even if I found the money, this place was so well guarded that there was no way I'd be able to sneak away without someone seeing me.

My life was over before I'd even had the chance to live.

"Why don't you take a shower and change before dinner."

It wasn't a suggestion. The temperature in the room felt like it'd dropped twenty degrees. I dragged my eyes up to Enzo's expressionless face. The man who stood before me was nothing like the man who'd just fucked me like it was the last time he was ever going to see me.

And that was when I understood. He'd acted that way because it was true. He wasn't going to fight for me. He was letting me go. That, or he knew, deep down, that he wouldn't be able to stop it. "So, that's it?" I asked him.

He cocked his head slightly in question.

"You're finished with me already?"

I searched his face for some sign of regret, anger...*something*. But there was nothing. And that made me angrier than anything he could've said.

"What about the things you promised me? The money? The ID? All the shit I'd need to start a new life. We made a deal, and I think I've more than lived up to it."

"I haven't forgotten," he said. "I just need time to figure out—for Luca and I to figure out—a way to get you those things without starting a war between the families. A war that we can't afford right now for numerous reasons."

I scoffed at his excuse. Even if that were true and he meant every word, he knew damn well there was no way they'd be able to buy time for me. Not now. Not when both Luigi and my father knew that I was here.

He was saying goodbye. That's what that sex fest had been about. He was saying goodbye.

His words meant nothing to me.

With a sigh, he squatted in front of me. Close enough to touch if I wanted him to. I didn't. "Sera," he said quietly. "I meant what I said when I promised to help you get away. But you have to understand, I'm stuck in a hard place right now, and all I'm asking is that you give me these few days to figure out a way to get you out of here without inciting your father. Will you do that for me?"

He was asking me to trust him with the impossible. But how did I trust a man I barely knew? A man who lied to me with his words when his eyes told me the truth?

But sitting here arguing with him was getting me nowhere, so I'd play along. For now. "Fine," I told him.

"Thank you," he said, and I could hear the relief in his voice. Tentatively, he brushed my hair back from my face, and I nearly burst into tears at the familiar gesture. "I promise we'll figure this out."

I nodded, not trusting myself to speak. Because no, we wouldn't. I knew my father. What Enzo was asking for would be impossible. There was no way I was going to escape. I never should have let him bring me here. I don't know what I was thinking, except that I hadn't wanted to stay in the hotel room by myself, or ask him to pay for it so that I could. And I had nowhere else to go without putting other people in danger.

With a heavy sigh, he gathered up his clothes that he'd folded so carefully in his suitcase and began hanging them up.

While he did that, I grabbed a bra and underwear, jeans, and an old Cure T-shirt from my own suitcase and headed into the shower. I couldn't even look at him right now. And if I wanted to have any chance of getting myself out of this situation, I needed to pull myself together and continue to act like the poor, helpless female who waited around while the men decided what they were going to do with her.

Yeah. Fuck that.

I'd get myself out of this situation.

Somehow.

Because there was no way in hell I was going back to my father without a fight.

CHAPTER 13

Enzo

I couldn't get Sera's face out of my head as I made my way downstairs before dinner to see if Luca had made any progress with his father. The hurt that dimmed the light in her eyes. The anger. The betrayal.

This was not how this was supposed to go. Dammit.

I wanted to run back up the stairs and drag her out of the shower and back into the bed. I wanted to hide from the rest of this fucked up world that was trying to tear us apart.

I wanted to stop time.

But no matter how much I wanted all of that, it wasn't going to happen. I couldn't hide and hope everything was just going to go away. Because sooner or later, the things that were trying to separate us would find us, and I needed to be prepared.

When I hit the bottom of the stairs, I pulled my sunglasses out of the inner pocket of my jacket and straightened my tie. It was black, as was my shirt and slacks. My usual attire when I was on duty.

When I arrived in Luca's office, he and Tristan were already there waiting for me, chatting quietly in the small sitting area in front of his desk. I nodded hello to them both and took my place beside Tristan.

Luca wasted no time in getting straight to the point. "I spoke with my father, and I was able to convince him to give us until the end of the week before he'll notify Ciro that we have his daughter. I told him I needed the time to get what information I could from her about her father and what he's doing up in Dallas, which I plan to do." He gave me a pointed look, and I held back the immediate denial that was on the tip of my tongue. He was right. She was a source of information and we needed to use her as such. When he saw I wasn't going to object, he continued what he was saying. "We have until Friday."

"That's only four days," I growled.

"I know," he told me. "And I'm sorry, my friend. That was the best I could do."

Tristan's quiet voice broke the tense silence that fell between us. "You shouldn't have gotten involved with her in the first place, Enzo." There was no judgement in his tone. The words were spoken only as fact, and nothing else.

I met his calm gaze, and, after an initial flash of anger that swiftly faded, I closed my eyes and took a deep breath. "You're right," I admitted. I turned back to Luca. "I should have brought her to you the instant I knew who she was. I shouldn't have hidden her from you. And I ask for your forgiveness for not trusting you. I was thinking with my cock instead of my head."

"Women have that effect on you sometimes." A small smile turned up one corner of Luca's mouth. Before Veda's appearance in his life, he would not have been so gracious about all of this. But I would never go so far as to say she'd made him soft. If anything, having her gave him more to protect. More to live for. And much less merciful to those who would threaten what he now had.

Restless, I rose from the couch and paced over to the window, my mind spinning as I searched for some way to change the course of my own actions. My heart began to race, and my lungs felt tight. I closed my eyes, fighting off the panic. "There's no way of getting her out of this, is there?" I asked after a moment.

"There is one," Luca said, and I tensed as I anticipated his words. "If you would just make an offer for her—"

"My answer is still no," I bit out.

"If you want to keep her, it's the only sensible solution," Tristan agreed.

"Who the fuck says I want to keep her?"

"Why else would you be acting this way?" he countered.

"And what way is that?"

"Like an overly possessive *stronzo*."

I wanted to deny it, but again, Tris was right. Still... "Marriage is a lifelong commitment. Not something I would ask of someone I've known all of a few weeks."

He shrugged one shoulder. "So divorce her when you tire of her. Or set her up in a nice condo downtown and live separate lives like most of the men in the family."

"I can't imagine myself ever growing tired of Sera." I hadn't meant to say the words aloud, but it was too late to take them back.

"Then marry her, Enzo," Luca insisted. "And I'm not going to sit here and lie to you about why I'm pushing you to do so. I want you to be happy, yes, but it would also provide us with the perfect opportunity to have an in with Ciro. If he goes off the deep end and decides to move into our territory, or we have the need to join forces with him in any way, it would give us a hell of a lot more bargaining power than we have now if his daughter is a member of our family. A way to avoid the inevitable violence that's in our future with him otherwise, if things keep going the way they do."

"What if he doesn't give a fuck about his daughter?"

Luca frowned. "He's a father. Perhaps not a good one, but a father nevertheless."

I came back over to the couch and sat down. "He's a father who's using his daughter as a bargaining chip to rise in power."

"As most mafia men do. So why shouldn't we take advantage of that? You've already taken the one thing from her that gave her any value."

"And he's not going to be happy about that."

"Marry her and it won't matter. She'll be protected."

I broke eye contact with Luca, feeling his and Tristan's heavy stare as I removed my sunglasses and rubbed the bridge of my nose. Keeping my eyes on the floor, I told them both, "I can't marry her. I won't do that to her. She deserves more."

"What do you mean by more?" Luca asked quietly.

Sliding my sunglasses back onto my face, I told him, "You know what I mean."

"Enzo, what happened with Alessandra—"

"Is exactly what will happen with Sera if I marry her."

"You don't know that."

"Yes, Luca. I do."

The room went silent until Luca said, "Then there's nothing for it. Once our four days are up, she goes back to her father." I felt his eyes on my face. "Are you going to be able to live with that, my friend?"

No. But I was going to have to. "Yes." The lie left a bitter taste in my mouth. A sourness I was getting more and more familiar with.

"Alright, then," Luca said after a moment. "I'll arrange the meeting with her father in four days' time. I suggest you get your head back in the game before then."

I gave him a nod. "Do you need me for anything else?"

"No," he said quietly. "I'll see you at dinner in an hour. Tomorrow morning you can bring Sera down here and we'll begin questioning her."

I felt strangely numb as I stood up from the couch and walked to the door with unhurried steps. The numbness continued once I was in the hall outside his office and didn't wear off until I was in the gym. I barely remembered getting there, but now I stood bare-knuckled in front of the punching bag wearing only gym shorts. Blood ran down my fisted hands in rivulets and dripped onto the mat I stood on with bare feet. Sweat stung my eyes and trickled down my spine.

Hauling back my right arm, I concentrated every ounce of rage that boiled in my blood into the punch I threw, hitting the bag so hard and fast it barely bounced. A left hook followed. Then the right again. Until I was punching the bag over and over as hard and fast as I could. When my knuckles were nothing but bloody, mangled meat, I started throwing knees and kicks.

My foot slipped in the blood, throwing me off balance. I fell forward, wrapping my arms around the punching bag to keep me upright. I hung on, my arms and legs shaking with fatigue as I struggled to regain my footing. When I did, I pushed the bag away from me with a violent shove, plowing my fist into it when it came back at me. Spittle flew from my mouth with every burning exhale.

Although physically I was at my limit, inside I was still screaming. And there was no one for me to blame but myself.

I never made it to dinner.

And no one came looking for me.

I showered in the small locker room at the gym, my bloody knuckles burning like a son of a bitch in the soapy water. But I suffered the pain as was my due for being such a *stronzo*. An asshole. Because that's what I was. I should've just let her leave that night she came to my door. I should've told Jade to warn her after Luca showed me her photo and told me who she was. By this time, she would be long gone.

And she would be free.

I didn't see Sera again until early the next morning when I caught her trying to sneak off the property before the sun came up.

LOVE ALL ANIMAL

CHAPTER 14

Serafina

Enzo never came to dinner and Luca was called away on an urgent matter ten minutes into our meal, so it was just Veda and I. She tried to talk Lisa, the one who'd made the delicious meal, into sitting and eating with us, but she refused, claiming she wanted to take advantage of the men's absence to tidy up Luca's office before she cleaned up the kitchen and finished up for the night.

Veda was quiet during our meal, but then again, so was I. My stomach was in knots, and I pushed my food around on my plate, unable to eat more than a few bites.

"I know what you're thinking."

I looked up in surprise to find Veda's eyes on me. "I'm sorry?"

She gave me a small smile. "I know what you're planning, Sera. And let me be the first to tell you, it's not going to work."

I didn't insult her intelligence by pretending not to know what she was alluding to. "It has to work. I can't stay here and wait for my father's men to show up to take me home."

"What makes you think Enzo will allow them to do that? Did he say something?"

I shook my head. "No. He told me he and Luca would figure something out."

"Well, there you go. You have nothing to worry about."

I set down my fork and sat back in my chair, giving up all pretense of eating. "Then why did he tell me goodbye this afternoon?"

Veda's smile fell from her face. "He said that?" she asked quietly.

"No. Not with words."

She stared at me, not understanding at first, before saying, "Oh."

"I tried to talk him into letting me go. But Luigi knows I'm here. There's no way he can do that without paying the consequences. And I understand that." Tears of frustration filled my eyes, and I stopped for a second to get myself together. "But I can't go back there, Veda."

"Can I ask why not? What's so bad about it at home?" Her tone was genuinely curious, but it shouldn't have surprised me. In the short time I'd known her, she'd never struck me as anything but down to earth and caring. So, I decided to be straight up with her.

"My father only cares about me in so far as the price he'll be paid for my innocent body."

She stared at me for a moment. "But are you? Innocent?"

"No," I told her. "Not anymore. And therein lies the problem. Because when my father gets me back home, he'll have his doctor examine me. And when he finds out I'm not a virgin anymore, I'll no longer have any value to him." And I honestly had no idea how he would react to that fact.

"How often does he check that?"

"Whenever he feels like there's a chance somebody's penis could've gotten too close to me." I shrugged. "So it was a daily experience there for a while. It was the price I had to pay to be able to go to school."

"Oh, my god. Sera! I'm so sorry." Reaching across the table, she touched my arm where it rested on the table. "There's something wrong with your fucking father."

I looked her dead in the eye and laughed. "There's something wrong with every man in the mafia. Haven't you figured that out yet? I can't imagine Luca is the image of virtue."

She gave me a look that said I had a point. "No, he's definitely not. But I think he really loves me. In his way."

I immediately felt bad for my sharp tone. "I think he does, too," I told her gently, and I meant it. Anyone with eyes could see how obsessed the man was with her.

A smile lit up her pretty face, and I smiled back. But then my own problems came crashing back. Placing my free hand over hers, I squeezed, my desperation coming through no matter how I tried to hold it in. "Will you help me, Veda? Please?"

She was shaking her head before I even got to the end of my question. "I can't, Sera. I'm so sorry. I couldn't betray Luca's trust like that. Besides," she added, "I don't know that there's anything I could do anyway."

"I'm not asking you to betray anyone," I insisted. "I'm just..." I didn't know what I was asking, exactly. "Could you tell me how to turn off the cameras? Or do you know anything about the schedule of the soldiers outside guarding the house? I'm just asking for a chance," I pleaded when she kept shaking her head.

Her eyes searched my face. "What about Enzo?"

The question hit me directly in the center of my chest. "What about him?"

Concern for her friend clouded her features. "He cares about you."

"He's giving me back to my father," I retorted.

She pulled her hand from my arm and sat back in her chair. "I don't believe that, Sera. I just can't. I've seen the way he looks at you. And look at everything he went through to get you out of Mexico."

Putting my elbows on the table, I rubbed my face with my hands and shoved my hair back from my face. "I'm telling you, there's nothing he could do, even if he wanted to."

"You have a few days," she insisted. "He and Luca will think of something."

This time it was my turn to shake my head. "No, Veda. You don't get it. You're not from this world. Luca will do what his father orders him to do. And Enzo will do what Luca tells him. It's the way they survive."

"There has to be something—"

"There's not."

She looked down at her hands, fingers laced together on the table in front of her empty plate. "I just can't believe he won't fight for you."

"I think he tried," I told her. Then I laughed softly as I looked away. "Or at least I like to think so." His words earlier that day came back to me. "But I think he's stuck in a hard place." I met her eyes. "You should understand something about this world you're living in, Veda."

"What's that?"

"These men"—my eyes swept the room, encompassing the entire house and everyone who was within it—"their loyalty to each other and to the family comes first. Before anything else. Before any*one* else. Luca loves you. He does," I assured her. "But if he had to choose between you and his mafia family, guess which one he would pick?"

"No," she whispered. "You're wrong."

"I'm sorry," I whispered back. "But it's true."

She frowned at me. "No," she insisted. "I don't believe Luca would do that to you. And I don't believe Enzo will do that to you. He genuinely cares for you. I can see it."

"Ask him what happened to Enzo's first wife," I told her. "Or ask Luca if you don't want to hear it firsthand. Then come back to me and tell me again how Luca would choose you."

"Enzo was married?"

I nodded.

"How do you know?"

"Everyone knows," I told her. "It's part of the reason he got a reputation that traveled all the way up to Dallas." And beyond.

"What do people say about him?"

I almost told her. I almost said the words out loud. But then I backed off. She might not believe me, but she would believe Luca—or Enzo—if they told her. "Just ask," I told her. "And then think about your decision not to help me. Either way, I don't plan to be here tomorrow." Sorrow filled me at losing this person who, I truly believed, would've become one of the best friends I'd ever had. "But I understand where you're coming from, and I won't blame you for it. So, all I'll ask is that you don't give me away."

She didn't respond, but I could tell by the look in her eyes that she wouldn't.

I stood up and took our plates to the sink, leaving my untouched meal to the side. "Is there any alcohol in this kitchen?"

"In the pantry over there," she said in a distracted tone. "There's some wine. Help yourself."

I opened the door and found a few bottles of some kind of pinot. I wasn't a wine expert, but honestly, I didn't really care what it was.

Taking one of the bottles, not bothering with a glass, I stopped when I got beside Veda. "Thank you for being so nice to me. I really like you, and I wish I didn't have to go."

She pushed back her chair and stood to give me a hug. "You don't have to," she insisted. "Please. Just hang around and give me a chance to talk to Luca and see what's going on."

I hugged her back as tight as I could with the bottle of wine dangling from one hand, and then released her. "I don't have time to wait. And if I'm going to get out of here, tonight is probably the only chance I'll have. The guys will be gone for a while and I'm sure Luca took some of his soldiers with him. Which means there are less men patrolling the property and lessons the chance of me being caught. Or shot." I tried to make light of it, but the joke fell flat.

Veda gave me a serious look, and I thought she'd try again to talk me out of it, but in the end, she only said quietly, "Be careful. And good luck. I'm going to be in the library for a bit working on a project for school and then I'll be in my room. The door will be closed, and I'll be watching something on TV."

"Thank you," I told her. "For everything." Leaving her in the kitchen, I made my way across the great room to the stairs. I didn't hurry. As a matter of fact, I made it a point to seem only as nervous as anyone would be as the new guest of the mafia underboss who was left to their own devices. I knew there were cameras throughout the house. Luca would be stupid not to have surveillance both outside and inside his home, and that man was definitely not stupid. However, they were hidden well. I'd only been able to locate a few of them—one in the kitchen while Veda and I ate, one in the hall outside my room, and one near the front door. As far as I knew, there weren't any in the bedrooms or bathrooms. So I had that going for me at least.

What I didn't know was how I was going to manage to sneak out with a suitcase. The answer was actually simple. I wasn't.

I didn't have any money, either. But what I did have was Enzo's watch that I'd tucked beneath my pillow earlier during our sex-filled afternoon. I wasn't an expert on watches, but it was a Rolex, so it had to be worth something. And judging by the tags on his suits and overall quality of everything he wore, it had to be worth a decent amount of money. Enough to get me the hell out of here. I'd worry about everything else once I was free of the threat of my father.

Six hours later, I sat on the edge of the bed in the bedroom. I'd added a thicker, long-sleeved fleece over my T-shirt and put sneakers on my feet. Enzo's watch was on my arm, and my coat was lying beside me on the mattress. I wasn't taking anything else. If I got caught trying to get off the property, I had a better chance of making the guards believe I had insomnia and got bored just being in the house if I didn't have a bag of clothes with me. They'd believe me. After all, I was just a woman. And every man knew women were ridiculous enough to do something like wander around outside at night by themselves without thinking they could be in danger.

Or, better yet, I could tell them I was looking for Enzo. That we'd had a fight or something. A few tears and it was guaranteed every man there would be too uncomfortable to question me farther.

Also, I didn't want anything on me that could identify me as the runaway daughter of Ciro Cordaro. My driver's license was staying here along with anything else that could tell people who I am. When I got to where I was going, I'd make up a name and a story and only work jobs that paid me under the table.

It would work.

So, why was I still sitting here?

Veda had come upstairs hours ago. I'd heard her door shut. The house was quiet. I had no idea when Enzo, Luca, and Tristan would get back, or how many guards remained outside, but it didn't matter. If I was very careful, I could get past them.

Taking a deep breath, I stood up and pulled on my coat. It had a hood that I'd use to cover my bright hair once I got outside. I glanced around the room one more time, blinking back the tears that were gathering in my eyes. Stupid, traitorous tears that dreamed of things that couldn't come true. Wiping them away with the back of my hands, I used the bathroom one last time and then I strode across the room and opened the bedroom door.

As quietly as I could, I made my way downstairs and out the patio doors. A cold, misty wind blew up around me as though the night itself was trying to tell me to turn back. But I couldn't. Not now.

The pool was lit with softly glowing lights that lit my way across the deck. To the right, a set of stairs disappeared into the dark. Stepping carefully as I lost the light from the pool, I made my way down into the darkness.

LOVE ALL ANIMALS

CHAPTER 15

Serafina

My eyes adjusted quickly to the dark, which was good, because the stairs were slick with the light drizzle of rain that was falling. When I reached the bottom, I found a latched gate and threw up a quick prayer that it wasn't padlocked because I really didn't want to have to try to climb over it.

Luckily, it opened easily. I closed it again as quietly as I could, just in case someone was lurking around, so nothing would look out of place. Then pulled up the hood of my coat over my hair, which I'd pulled back into two braids to avoid any strands slipping out and giving me away. Something rustled in the brush to my left and I froze. But whatever it was, it must've run away.

I knew my escape was being caught on Luca's security cameras, but I was banking on the fact that by the time someone noticed I was gone, the only thing they'd see is me walking off the property. I planned to head one direction and then double back to try to throw them off as to which direction I'd gone.

I looked up, squinting my eyes against the drizzly rain. Luca's house clung to the edge of the rock formation that rose a good thirty or forty feet above me. From where I stood, the ground sloped steeply down to the lake. If I slipped, I could only hope that I could catch myself on one of the scraggly trees before I slid all the way down.

I thought about that for a second. Maybe escape by water would be the way to go. I seriously doubted there were any guards patrolling the side of a hill like that. But then I dismissed the idea. It was too cold, and I didn't have any dry clothes. I'd stick to my original plan and hope for the best.

Carefully, I followed the narrow trail of even ground that hugged the bottom of the outcropping of rock Luca's house was built on. My plan was to find the driveway at the front of the house and then follow it out to the gate while staying under the cover of the trees that covered the property. That way, if I saw anyone, I could easily step out onto the drive and use whatever excuse for being there I thought would work best. If I was found too far from the drive, it would be way too obvious that I was trying to sneak out. Plus, I didn't know how much land Luca owned, but I would bet my life that the perimeter was protected by a wall and guards.

By the time I saw the lights from the front of the house and the paved drive, my thighs were burning from slipping and sliding on the wet ground as I climbed up the hill. Outside the circle of light, I stopped by a tree for a few seconds and caught my breath. All three of the SUVs were gone, but I made myself wait, listening for guards. When I didn't hear anything, I pushed away from the tree and started following the drive away from the house. I kept my hands in my pocket and my head down, hoping my dark hoodie and jeans would keep me hidden in the dark. As I walked, I scanned the area around me as discreetly as I could.

My heart was beating so hard now I could barely hear anything around me as I blinked the moisture out of my eyes. I wished I'd checked the weather before I left, but then thought it wouldn't have mattered anyway. Tonight was my only chance, and I had to take it. If the skies decided to open up and drench me in a typical Texas rainfall, then that's just the way it was going to be. And maybe the rain was working to my favor. No one would expect anyone to be out and about in this shit.

I took a quick look to either side of me. So far, I hadn't seen anyone patrolling the grounds. Had they all gone with Luca? That would be a stroke of luck I'd never expected, and would make my life so much easier. By the time they got back to the house, I'd be long gone.

Hopefully.

I was cold and damp, but after a few more minutes my nerves began to calm and I quickened my pace, not worrying so much about how much noise I was making. It didn't seem like anyone was around to hear it. At least not until I got to the gate. Luca wouldn't have left that unprotected. And I had no idea how I was going to get past them, but I'd figure it out when I got there.

It was really dark now where I was. No moon or anything to help light my way. But I wasn't afraid of the dark. The dark kept me hidden. It kept me safe.

An ancient oak tree with a trunk wider than my body suddenly loomed in front of me and I corrected my direction to go around it. Only before I could, something hard and heavy slammed into me from behind.

My hands came out of my pockets and flew out in front of me to try to catch myself before I hit the wet bark, but I wasn't in time. The air rushed out of me in a whoosh! as I hit the tree, turning my head just in time to avoid smashing my nose. The side of my face scraped along the bark, and I hissed in pain.

A man's large hand was plastered to the tree right beside my face, the knuckles wrapped in white bandages. A dark stain seeped through the cotton. Blood, I would imagine. A hard body pressed into my back, and I could feel his cock stiffening against my ass. A gravelly voice in my ear raised the hair on the back of my neck.

"After everything I fucking did for you, you're going to betray me like this?"

I almost laughed out loud. "Betray *you*?" I asked incredulously. "You're about to turn me over to my father." I practically spit the words at him. "When you promised me...you *promised* me... that you wouldn't. So, who is betraying who here, Enzo?"

He pulled my hood from my head and pressed his cheek to the side of my face that wasn't against the tree trunk. I could feel him trembling. His entire body shook against mine, and instinctively I wanted to try to soothe him. But then I remembered why we were in this position.

Frustration filled me as I tried to buck him off of me. I'd been so close to freedom. So fucking close. "Why are you still here?" I gritted out. "Why aren't you with Luca?"

"Because I can't stand to be away from you," he whispered. "Not now."

Kind of hard to believe when I hadn't seen him since that afternoon when he fucked me into exhaustion. "Then where have you been all night?"

"Watching you."

Maybe I should've felt more surprised than I did. Maybe I should've felt angrier that I was caught before I could get away. But I didn't feel either of those things. Instead, as the tension drained from my body, I felt such an overwhelming sense of relief that I could've cried.

But what I felt didn't matter. What I wanted in my heart of hearts didn't matter. I couldn't stay here with him, no matter how much I wanted to. To stay would only be delaying our inevitable separation. It might buy us a few more days together, but in the end, we'd still be apart, and I would be back at my father's. A prisoner. And there was no way I'd escape him a second time. "Just let me go," I told him.

Instead of answering me, he pushed his hips harder into my ass. I closed my eyes as my body responded with a rush of moisture between my thighs. I wanted to turn around in his arms and let him take me back to the house. But even as my body vibrated with need, my head screamed at me to run. To get away.

He rolled his hips into me again, and his breathing quickened, becoming fast and harsh.

"No," I lied. "I don't want you. I don't want this."

I felt him stiffen against my back, and I continued on, knowing I was hurting him, but also knowing I had no choice. "The only thing I wanted from you was your money so I could buy my freedom." I paused, waiting to see what he would do. But he didn't ease up the pressure of his weight against me. "I don't *want* you," I gritted through my teeth. "Just let me go, Enzo."

Seconds ticked by with agonizing slowness. I started to worry I'd gone too far. But then, suddenly, he pushed himself off of me. I sucked in a deep breath of cold air and braced myself to face him. To make him believe the lies that were coming out of my mouth.

I never got the chance.

His arms came around my waist, and before I knew it, he had my jeans unfastened and was tugging them down my hips along with my underwear. Cold, wet air hit my bare ass, and I grabbed ahold of the front of my jeans, trying to stop their descent. "What are you doing?" Panic made my voice higher than normal. "Enzo. Stop!"

He shoved his hand between my legs and cupped me from behind, sliding his fingers between my folds. "You don't want me?" he growled when he felt how wet I was. "You're a fucking liar."

My strength was no match for his, and soon my pants were down around my knees, and I was once again pressed against the tree with his hand on my head to hold me there as he opened his slacks. I struggled against him with everything I had in me, feeling the bark scrape my cheek and the front of my thighs. I tried to hit him, but my punches were ineffectual. I couldn't land anything in the position I was in. And my legs were trapped in my jeans. Now I was starting to get really pissed off. "Stop!" I shouted, louder this time. "I'll scream!"

"Go ahead and scream," he told me. "I'll let them fucking watch."

No, he wouldn't.

"Try me, baby girl."

Sucking in a breath, I screamed as loud as I could as he chuckled in my ear and shoved his thick cock between my thighs. I pushed my hips forward against the tree as much as I could to try to escape him, but he only groaned as he slid out before he pulled my hips back again. I gasped as he worked his way between the folds of my sex until his cock was as slick as I was.

I heard men shouting from every direction and I froze, realizing what an idiot I'd been. "Enzo, please. Don't do this."

"You think it would really be this easy to escape from Luca's property?" he asked me as he continued to rock his hips back and forth, sliding his sex in and out of the folds of my pussy.

Through the haze of lust taking over my body, the truth came crashing over me. He'd told them to let me go. While he hunted me himself.

Running footsteps drew closer, and I tried again to play off his possessiveness. "All of Luca's soldiers are about to see my bare ass."

But he only said, "All of Luca's soldiers are about to watch me fuck you."

I renewed my efforts to get away just as six men came upon us from different directions. The ones I could see froze, lowering their weapons when they saw what was happening. "Help me!" I screamed at them, but not one of them stepped forward to do so. Stone faced, they waited for orders from Enzo.

Tired of my games, Enzo yanked me away from the tree and threw me forward. Caught up in my jeans, I stumbled and fell, landing hard on my hands and knees. One hand slipped in the wet grass, and I barely caught myself before I face planted.

"You and you. Turn around," Enzo growled, and at first, I thought he was talking to me, but he was talking to his men. "But don't leave. Keep an eye out. The rest of you can watch."

Rolling over onto my back, I started tugging my jeans back up. But they were wet and stuck to my skin. Before I could make much progress, Enzo was on his knees, flipping me back over. I clawed at the ground, trying to crawl away. An angry sob caught in my throat. I wanted to hate him. Hate what he was doing to me. But I was so tuned into him, to his touch, even as rough as it was, that I couldn't do either of those things.

He grabbed my hips with both hands.

"Enzo." I glared at him over my shoulder with fire-filled eyes. "If you do this, I'll never fucking forgive you."

His dark eyes met mine, but they were nothing but pools of blackness in the dark mist. I felt the head of his cock nudging my entrance, and then he forced his way inside of me with one strong thrust. My arms buckled at the force of his thrust, but didn't give out. He didn't give me any time to adjust to him before he started slamming into me hard and fast, his body bent over mine, one hand hitting the ground beside my head and the other digging into my hip, pulling me back to meet him. He wasn't gentle. He never was. But this was more than just sex. This was his way of controlling me. Of controlling the situation. Of taking out his anger because he couldn't actually control either.

I knew this somewhere deep inside, and yet I couldn't stop the ache in my chest from spreading that he was treating me this way, or the burn of mortification that he was doing it in front of his men. And yet my traitorous body took him hungrily inside of me, loving the way his thick length stretched me almost to the point of pain. Tension filled my womb, sparks of pleasure shooting through me with every thrust. I clenched my teeth, refusing to give into the pleasure.

"You're mine," he growled between harsh breaths. "Capisci cazzo, donna?" *Do you fucking understand, woman?* "You don't leave me until I say you do."

I didn't answer. I didn't think he was really expecting one, and I wasn't about to argue with him when he was obviously out of his fucking mind. Tears burned the back of my eyes, making them burn, but I refused to let them fall. I refused to let him see how much he was hurting me.

He thrust hard, pushing as deep as he could go. I felt him swell inside of me and heard him cry out as he came, a raw sound that tore at my heart, his come filling me until it leaked out around the sides of his cock and ran down the insides of my thighs. His weight was heavy on my back as he tucked his face into the back of my neck, muffling the sounds he made.

When it was done, I stayed silent and still as I waited for him to get off of me. My face and thighs stung where the tree bark had abraded my skin and from the corner of my eye I saw one of his men rub his palm down the front of his pants. Mortification filled me as Enzo's lips pressed against the back of my neck, exposed by my braids falling to either side, and a chill ran down my spine. And then I felt his hand—the one that was on my hip—slide around to dip between my legs...

Immediately, I began to struggle. "No. No!"

His other arm came around my throat and he straightened, taking me with him until we were on our knees with my back against his front. He was still inside of me. I dug my fingers into his arm, trying to pull it away, but I couldn't make him budge. All around us, Luca's soldiers watched as Enzo shoved my jeans further down my legs and his fingers found me. "All of these men are going to watch you come," he told me. "Hear you scream my name."

"Fuck you! I won't," I swore.

He chuckled, but the sound was dark and cold. "You will."

I tried to shake my head, to deny it, but a moan escaped my lips as he tightened his hand around my throat and pushed his finger inside of me alongside his cock, wetting it and sliding it up to my clit.

"So wet," he whispered. "So sweet. I want to taste you on my tongue, baby. Your mouth. Your skin. Your cunt." He pressed the heel of his hand into my lower stomach and rolled his hips. I felt him harden inside of me again. Delicious tension tightened and released low in my belly as he played me like a fine instrument, knowing exactly when to add pressure and when to ease off. In the short time we'd known each other, he'd learned my body better than I knew it myself. And no matter how hard I tried to fight it, to deny him, my body begged for release.

"I hate you," I whispered.

"No, you don't."

He shoved two fingers inside of me, stretching me wide, sliding them in and out with his cock, and I sucked in a breath. I wasn't cold anymore. As a matter of fact, I wanted nothing more than to strip off my coat and the rest of my clothes and writhe naked in the mud in front of these men.

"Unzip your coat and lift your shirt. I want to see you touch your breasts." His voice was low. Commanding.

A tear slid down my face, my body moving, straining toward the pleasure his fingers promised. I was about to deny him, but I knew it wouldn't matter. He would still get what he wanted, one way or the other. I let go of his arm and unfastened my jacket and raised my shirt and pulled down the cups of my bra, exposing my bare breasts to the damp, wet air and the hungry eyes that silently watched us.

"Touch yourself, Sera."

My head fell back against his shoulder as I found my nipples, hard and sensitive in the cold air.

"Show me what you like."

His fingers were still inside of me with his cock, his thumb slowly circling my clit. With shaking hands, I palmed my breasts, giving them a squeeze before I took my nipples between my thumb and forefinger and tweaked them hard then pulled, encouraging them to get harder still as I rolled them between my fingers.

"Thank you," he said, his voice strained. As my reward, he moved his fingers back to my clit and imitated what I'd done with my nipples.

I cried out as the tight waves of pleasure deep in my womb intensified, growing closer and stronger.

"My name," he growled. "Say it."

I didn't want to obey him. But it didn't matter. "Enzo!"

I felt his entire body shudder. "Tell me what you want."

"Please."

"Please what, baby girl?"

"Please make me come," I whispered.

"I can't hear you."

"Make me come," I cried. "Please, Enzo!"

"Good girl." His fingers dove inside of me again and then he was back at my clit. He whispered in my ear, telling me how beautiful I was and how much he wanted me. How he wanted to fuck me everywhere, so there wouldn't be a single inch of me that didn't know him. "But right now, I want to watch you come, Sera. I want to feel you squeezing my cock and fall apart in my arms."

I whimpered at his words. I was so close.

"Come for me NOW."

My body responded as if it was only waiting for his command, the pain and pleasure of it too much, and I cried out his name as he demanded. His hand tightened around my neck until I couldn't breathe, but holy fuck. And I decided right then and there that if I was going to die, this was the way I wanted to go.

He released me and I fell forward onto my hands and knees, waves of pleasure still shooting through me. Enzo gripped my hips and pumped in and out with strong, deep strokes, coming inside of me again as my climax still shuddered through my body.

As I fought to catch my breath, he pulled out of me and lifted me from the ground back onto my knees. Gently, he fixed my bra and pulled down my shirt, then helped me to my feet. "You won't run from me again," he said quietly as he got my underwear and jeans back up. He didn't bother to fasten them.

I felt his eyes on my face, but I couldn't look at him. My lower half felt wet and sticky inside my jeans. A reminder of what had just happened. Rage and humiliation burned inside of me, but I didn't dare act on it, lest one of his guards react in a way that wouldn't turn out well for me.

"Leave us." He shouted the order to the men, and they immediately dispersed, going back to their posts. Probably to jack off.

Hurt and humiliation washed over me. I wanted to sink into the ground and bury myself in the wet earth. I wanted to hurt him as he'd hurt me.

"Sera."

I wondered how far I would get if I made a run for it. Probably not far.

"Sera, look at me."

I shook my head. I couldn't. I'd never be able to look at him again.

He grabbed my chin and forced my head up. "Open your eyes and LOOK at me, or so help me God, I'll—"

I lost it then.

My fists came up, and I flailed at him, hitting him everywhere I could as the dam broke, and angry tears burst forth, obscuring my vision. I couldn't see. I couldn't hear anything but the ringing in my ears. I screamed and cursed. And hit him. Over and over and over until my voice was nothing but a raw whisper and my fists and arms were tired and sore.

When there was nothing left inside of me, I dropped my arms to my sides and took an exhausted breath.

"I deserved that this time," Enzo said quietly. "But if you ever raise a hand to me again, I'll—"

"You'll what?" I demanded dully as I stared down at the ground between us. "Rape me in front of your men?" I couldn't keep the venom from my voice.

He was quiet for a long time. "Sera," he said quietly. "Look at me. Please."

Fighting back tears, I slowly raised my eyes to his, and a fresh wave of pain exploded inside of me when I saw the horror and determination in his at what he'd done.

CHAPTER 16

Enzo

I stared down into the oceans of pain and humiliation that dominated Sera's perfect face. One side was scraped and bloodied from the tree trunk. I lifted my hand to touch her without thinking about it, horrified that I'd hurt her, then let it fall to my side again. Her screams echoed in my ears, a haunting reminder of the past, and my jaw hurt where she'd landed a good punch.

For a moment, my throat was so tight I couldn't speak.

What the fuck was wrong with me?

I'd spotted Sera on the video feed the moment she'd left our bedroom. I'd known immediately that she was leaving. She was running.

My first thought was that I should let her go.

I called the soldiers patrolling the grounds outside and ordered them to stand down. To ignore her. And told them I would handle her myself.

She'd made it around the bottom of the cliff and halfway to the road before I jumped up from the desk and went after her. And when I found her...

I simply lost my fucking mind.

Even as I admired her determination and self-reliance, a god-awful rage filled me that she would dare to disobey me. That she'd put her life in danger like that. I knew the anger I'd displayed was just a mask disguising the anguish I felt that she wanted to leave me. So much so that she'd go with no clothes. No money. No weapons.

She stared up at me now with pain in her eyes. So much fucking pain. Something cracked wide in my chest when she asked in a horrified whisper, "How could you do that to me?"

"You ran from me," I told her. Like that was any excuse. But I wouldn't apologize. I couldn't. Because I wasn't sorry for what I'd done. Living on her own had made her forget just how dangerous this life was. I'd done nothing but given her a reminder. She was lucky it was me who found her, and not some whack job on the street. Or a gang of them.

"Are you really surprised, Enzo?" she asked bitterly as she wiped at her face, wincing when she accidentally touched the scrapes on her cheek. "What the hell would you do in my situation?"

"I would keep my word and give me a fucking chance to fix this."

"Fix it?" she asked. Then she laughed. "There is no fixing it. You said so yourself. You only have two choices here: Give me back to my father or start a war. That's it." She paused, and her eyes glinted with determination when they met mine. "Or you could give me my money and let me go," she said quietly.

"No," I told her. "I won't do that." I couldn't do that. Because something told me that if I did, I would never see her again. And that was unacceptable to me. If she was with her father, I would know where she was. I would know what happened to her.

A few strands of her hair had come loose from her braids, and I brushed them back off her face. Her hair was wet, and her skin was cold. "Let's go back to the house."

She took a quick step back. "I can't go back there."

I frowned. "Sera—"

"How the hell do you expect me to *ever* go back there after what you just did?" she asked. She threw one hand in the air, gesturing in the general direction of the house. "Hell, Luca and Tristan and who the hell knows who else are probably enjoying the show you just put on as we speak." She glanced up at the trees. "Oh, my god." She speared me with a horrified look. "There're cameras out here, aren't there? Not just around the house."

Of course, there were. "I'll delete the footage. And no one is watching."

She lifted her chin in an attempt to hang onto her pride as her lovely mouth twisted into a sneer. "What about the guards who had a front-row seat?"

"No one will dare to say anything to you. And if they do, I'll kill them." And I meant it.

She stilled as she stared up at me. "I don't want you to kill them."

"Fine. I'll have them reassigned."

"They'll talk."

"I'll cut out their fucking tongues first."

I was dead serious, and she knew it. Her mouth snapped shut. She stared at me as if she'd never seen me before tonight. And perhaps she hadn't. But she sure as hell was seeing me now. "Come on. We're going back to the house."

"No." She shook her head. "I'm not going back. I'm leaving." She started to back away, watching me warily to see if I would still give chase.

I sighed. "You're not going anywhere, Sera. So you can either walk back to the house with me before we get soaked out here, or I'll forcibly drag you back. But either way, you're returning with me now so we can get you cleaned up and into some dry clothes."

Her eyes hardened, and she lifted her chin in that stubborn gesture I was starting to know well.

But I wasn't in the mood. "You won't win this fight, baby girl. Not this time." I crossed my arms over my chest and waited. If she wanted to drag this out, fine, we could do that. But she wasn't going to win. I *couldn't* let her win. Because to do so would mean letting her go. And I wasn't ready to do that.

She studied my expression for a few seconds, searching for cracks in my armor, and when she didn't find any her shoulders dropped as the tension visibly drained from her and she averted her eyes. "I don't want to go back to my father."

The hopelessness in her voice tore at something inside of me. Something I thought was long dormant. I dropped my arms back down to my sides. She looked so small and helpless in that moment that I wanted nothing more than to wrap her in my arms and swear that I would protect her from her father and anyone else who tried to harm her. But it would be another lie, because I wouldn't be able to protect her from myself. And besides, I knew she wouldn't accept that from me. Not at this moment. "I know," I told her.

She sniffed and looked away again. I could see her shivering.

I took a step toward her. Stopped. "Come back to the house with me. Let me take care of you."

That stubborn chin of hers dropped in defeat, and it broke my heart to see it. But I needed to get her inside and cleaned up before Luca and Tristan got home. "Okay," she whispered so softly I barely heard her. I held out my hand, but she ignored it completely as she walked around me and started toward the glow of lights from the house.

Breathing a sigh of relief, I followed her, knowing this docile act was only temporary.

As we approached the circular driveway in front of the house, I pulled my sunglasses out of my inside jacket pocket and put them on. One of the guards standing by the front door was having a smoke as he scanned the trees surrounding the drive. It wasn't one of the men who'd come running earlier, but I still saw Sera's steps falter when she noticed him standing there.

Taking her arm, I propelled her toward the front door before she could try to run. The guard glanced over at us when we approached. With one look, he took in our wet clothes and the scrapes on Sera's face. "Everything okay?" he asked.

"Everything is fine," I told him. "Any word from Luca?"

"Not yet."

"Let me know if you hear anything," I said as I opened the front door and led Sera inside.

"Yes, sir." He pulled the door closed behind us. I released her arm once we were inside and followed her through the house.

Veda came out of her room just as we reached the top of the stairs. She took one look at Sera's face and went into panic mode. "Holy shit! Sera! What happened?" Running up to her, she took her by the shoulders and tried to look at Sera's face as Sera tried to hide it. Only Veda was having none of it and it didn't work. She sent me a furious look. "What did you do?"

"Go back to your room, Veda," I told her firmly.

Her eyes narrowed. "I'm not going anywhere until Sera tells me she's okay."

"I'm okay," Sera told her. "Seriously, I am. I just...tripped in the dark and fell into a tree."

I noticed she didn't try to explain to Veda what she was doing outside at night in the rain, which meant Veda knew damn well what was going on. Something I'd talk to her about later.

"Are you sure?" Veda asked her.

"Yeah," Sera said. "I just want to take a bath and go to bed."

Veda didn't seem completely convinced. She glanced at me, then back at Sera, before finally giving in. "Okay. If you need anything, just yell. Do you want a cup of tea or something?"

"That would be great," Sera told her. "Thanks."

"I'll bring it to your room," Veda told her. With another unreadable look at me, she left to go get the tea.

"Come on," I told Sera.

In our room, I walked over to the closet and took off my sunglasses and my jacket, watching Sera as she passed me and went straight into the bathroom. Her movements were stiff as she stripped off her wet coat and dropped it on the tile floor, then kicked off her shoes. She was careful not to look at me as she sat on the side of the tub and turned on the water, but I could see the tense set of her jaw and the flush to her cheeks.

There was a knock at the door, and I told Veda to come in. She entered cautiously, holding a steaming cup of tea for Sera.

I came out into the bedroom and lifted my chin toward the bathroom. "She's in there," I told her. As she went to walk by me, I took her arm. "You knew what she was doing, and you didn't stop her. Why?"

She looked up at me. "Did you hurt her?" she asked quietly.

"Answer my question, Veda."

"Answer mine, Enzo."

Veda and I had gotten comfortable with each other in the time she'd been Luca's guest here in the house. I was her guard. I trained her in self-defense. I watched out for her. But right now, she was staring at me like she had no idea who I was. The same look Sera had given me earlier, and I was surprised by how much it bothered me. I removed my hand from her arm. "No," I told her. "Not intentionally." Not physically.

After a moment, she told me, "I knew she planned to try to leave tonight. I chose to shut myself in my room. I didn't see anything."

"Why did you do that? She could've been hurt."

Her expression darkened. "Because no matter how happy I might be now, I remember how terrified I was when Luca first brought me here."

"Does she seem terrified to you?"

Her eyes softened as she glanced toward the bathroom door. "Maybe not of you, but she *is* terrified." She paused. "Be careful with her, Enzo," she warned. "Or you're going to lose her. One way or the other."

I was about to tell her that what happened with Sera and I wasn't her business, but she was right. "Go ahead and give her the tea. And then give us some privacy, please."

Her eyes traveled over my face. Whatever she was looking for, she must've found it. "I'll just be a minute."

Partway to the bathroom she stopped and turned partially toward me. "Have you heard anything from Luca?"

"Not yet," I answered. "But I'm sure he's fine."

"Yeah." She gave me an unsteady smile. She didn't seem convinced.

"He's fine, Veda. He always is. And Tristan is with him."

She glanced down at the floor and took a breath, then nodded and took Sera her tea. When she came back, she said, "She told me to tell you to stay the hell out." One eyebrow lifted. "I don't suppose you'll listen to her request?"

One corner of my mouth lifted in a smile. "I'm glad she's feeling more like herself." I walked over to the door and held it open for her. "Goodnight, Veda. I'll let you know if I hear from Luca. But no news is good news in these kinds of situations. I'm sure he'll be home in a few hours."

"I hope you're right. Goodnight, Enzo. Don't be an ass."

Once she was gone, I closed and locked the door behind her, then stripped off my shirt and dropped it near my jacket in the closet. I kicked off my shoes and took off my pants, boxer briefs, and socks. Naked, I walked into the bathroom.

Sera's wet clothes were in a pile near the sink, and I spotted my watch on the counter. So that's how she was going to support herself. Smart girl.

She was just lowering herself into the tub, her mouth twisted in pain as she carefully got into the water. I immediately saw why. The front of her thighs were scraped and bloody like her face. "Jesus Christ."

She didn't even bother to look over at me as she finally got herself settled and leaned back, closing her eyes. "I see you ignored my message."

"You shouldn't be surprised."

She sighed, her voice full of resignation as she said, "I'm not."

With my hand on the back of her head, I sat her forward and got into the water behind her.

"What are you doing?" Though there was a thread of annoyance in her tone, mostly she just sounded so very tired.

"I'm cold." The sides of her throat flushed red, and I knew she was thinking of the last bath we'd taken together. The night I'd taken her virginity. "Relax," I told her as I leaned back and pulled her against my chest. "I'm just trying to get warm."

Water sloshed over the sides as I wrapped my arms around her. Over her shoulder, I could see the bath water tinged red from the blood on her thighs. "I'm so sorry I hurt you," I said quietly in her ear. "I didn't realize the tree bark was so rough."

"I tried to tell you to stop." Her voice was small, and it hurt me to hear it.

"You didn't tell me you were hurt," I countered, trying—and failing—to ignore the pang of guilt that went through me. "Don't ever not tell me." I tightened my arms around her. "I know I can be...insistent sometimes. Even rough. But you need to tell me if it's too much. You can always tell me, Sera."

She was quiet for a minute. And then she said, "I honestly didn't think you'd care. No one else ever has."

I knew exactly who she was referring to. "I'm not your father," I told her. "I may not be a gentle man, baby girl, but I'm not him. I would never intentionally hurt you like this."

"I believe you," she said after a moment.

She was quiet as we soaked in the water, and I was all talked out myself. I was fucking exhausted. I hadn't been sleeping well since Sera was taken. Even after I'd gotten her back, I tended to only doze here and there, waking up often to reassure myself that she was still there. The sleepless nights were catching up to me, which was the reason Luca had me stay back this time.

Well, one of the reasons. The other was falling asleep in my arms, her lips parted and her breathing deep and even.

I found a washcloth draped over the side of the tub and dipped it into the bathwater, then I adjusted her so she was leaning against my right shoulder and I could see her face where the bark had scraped up her skin. Her eyes popped open, and she sucked in a hissing breath as I started to wash the dirt and blood away.

"This needs to be cleaned," I murmured.

She said nothing as I dipped the cloth back into the water and added some soap.

"This is gonna sting, but I have some salve and I'll help you get bandaged up before we go to bed."

"Okay. Thank you." She was quiet while I finished washing her face and made sure the dirt had soaked out of the scrapes on her thighs. As I helped her out of the tub and wrapped her up in a towel, she asked me, "Do you really think you'll be able to get me away from my father?"

No. Not at all. But I sure as hell wasn't going to tell her that. Wrapping my towel around my waist, I sighed heavily and ran a hand through my own wet hair. Some perverse masochistic part of me wanting to know... "I need to ask you something, Sera."

She was standing in front of the sink looking at the damage to her face. Her eyes met mine in the mirror. Tension pulsed between us. The same energy that was always there. It poked and prodded at the shell I'd built around my heart, searching for a way in.

"Do you really want to leave me?" My heart sped up as I waited for her answer. "If tonight hadn't happened, and we could find a way out of this, would you still want to be free? Of me?"

She started to respond, then stopped. I opened and closed my hands as I waited for her answer, fighting down the panic that was trying to rise inside of me. "Honestly?" she asked.

I gave her a nod.

Slowly, she turned to face me. "No," she said quietly. "I don't know." The tears that had been gathering in the corners of her blue-gray eyes spilled over. "And I'm probably the sorriest excuse for women's rights in the entire universe, but even after what you did to me tonight, I don't want to leave you."

Relief flooded my veins, so fast and hard it made me sway on my feet. And not even her next words could damper it.

"But I have to. I can't stay here, Enzo. I can't stay with you. Eventually he'd come for me. You won't be able to stop him. Not because he loves me, but because it would be a blow to his pride that you managed to steal something from him. Because that's all I am to him. A bargaining chip to further his own agenda."

I stared down at this woman who had taken my world and upended it with nothing but her gap-toothed smile, and the words were coming out of my mouth before I could stop them. "He can't have you. Not anymore."

The way she looked at me made me wonder if what I heard in my head and what I'd said were two different things.

"What?" I asked her. "Why are you looking at me that way?"

She opened her mouth to speak, and then closed it again and shook her head. "Nothing."

"Tell me."

Her mouth twisted into something sour. "There's only one way he'll ever agree to let you keep me. And that's only if his return on investment is worth it." A nervous laugh burst from her. "Of course, I'm no longer a virgin. The one thing he valued about me and that he could use to sell to a higher bidder. So perhaps you'd have a chance."

I knew what she was talking about. "I can't marry you, Sera. That isn't an option."

There was a flash of hurt in her eyes before she quickly turned back to the mirror and started taking her hair down.

"It has nothing to do with you."

"It has everything to do with me," she countered. Picking up my brush, she started ripping it through her hair with rough strokes. "It's my life, Enzo. It has *everything* to do with me. But if you don't want me..." She trailed off, swallowing hard.

"Sera."

"There's nothing I can do about that," she finished.

I came up behind her and took the brush from her hand before she ripped out all of her hair. Carefully, I started working out the knots, my heart in my throat from memories of doing this for Alessandra. "I never said I didn't want you."

"But you don't want me enough to marry me."

Setting down the brush, I leaned back against the sink and pulled her around until she was standing between my thighs. "I know you won't understand, but it's safer for you that way."

There was something in her eyes as she stared up at me. Something I didn't at first understand.

"Okay," she finally said.

And it was then that I understood.

She knew.

She knew what happened with Alessandra. "Sera, you need to understand—"

"I do understand. I know you. You're a mafia man. And you always will be. You represent the exact thing I'm trying to get away from."

"That's not all I am," I confessed. "I'm also a man. A man who doesn't want to lose you."

"I know."

A trickle of cold sweat slithered down my spine as I bent to softly kiss her lips.

LOVE ALL ANIMAL

CHAPTER 17

Serafina

The following morning, Enzo brought me into Luca's office. The underboss sat behind his desk, papers spread out before him. He looked up when we entered, then stood, buttoning his jacket as he did so. He wore a tailored black suit, as did Enzo, only his shirt was white and he wore no tie.

"Please, come in," he told us. "Enzo, close the door behind you. Sit." He gestured to the couch in front of his desk, removing a large book from one of the cushions and setting it on the glass coffee table. As I approached, I saw that it looked to be an English Literature textbook. One of Veda's, I gathered.

I sat down closest to the desk where the book had been, and Enzo unbuttoned his suit jacket and sat beside me.

Luca did the same, taking the chair across from us. I tried not to appear nervous, but to be honest, I couldn't help it. I was putting my life in the hands of these two men.

Luca's eyes ran over the scraped side of my face, already looking better than it had last night thanks to the ointment Enzo had carefully applied before we got into bed, and sent Enzo a questioning look.

"It wasn't intentional."

His answer seemed to satisfy him. "I was wondering if you would help me," Luca said to me.

"That depends," I told him. "What do you need help with?"

His blue eyes were calculating. "Your father, of course."

I glanced at Enzo, but his attention was on his boss.

Luca sat back in the chair and crossed his ankle over his knee. "What can you tell me about your father, Sera?"

My guard shot up immediately, more out of habit than any real need to protect my father. I shrugged. "What do you want to know? And I'll let you know if I can tell you or not."

His gaze assessed me and left me feeling cold. "I suggest you decide quickly where your loyalty lies. With your father, who, by your own words, cares very little for you, or with the man who cared about you enough that he risked his own life to save you from a life of forced prostitution. And therefore, by extension, me."

He was right. And I owed my father nothing. "My father is a mafia man," I told him. "He wants what every mafia man wants: Money. Power. Control." Again, I glanced at Enzo. I couldn't help myself. He was so calm beside me, one arm over the back of the couch where I sat but not touching me. He gave me a nod of encouragement, and I turned back to Luca. "He wants to control all of Texas. And then the world."

"That's not going to happen," he responded. "What else can you tell me? What do you know about his activities in Dallas?"

"Specifically?"

"Yes."

"Not very much," I told him. "I'm sorry. Surprisingly enough, I wasn't included in those conversations." The sarcasm was thick in my voice.

Again, his blue eyes studied me, and I had the feeling he was delving directly into my mind to catch me in any lies. "There was nothing you overheard? Nothing at all you can give me?"

I shook my head. "No. I'm sorry. I swear I would tell you if I did. Mostly because you terrify me, to be completely honest." Enzo's hand squeezed my shoulder. I took a bracing breath. "But I was confined to my room the majority of the time when I was home. My father was very careful around me when it came to his schemes. I don't think he trusted me." I let out a sharp laugh. "Probably the smartest thing he ever did."

Luca released a sigh and leaned forward in his chair, bracing his elbows on his knees, his expression thoughtful.

Enzo touched my jaw with his fingertips. "Are you absolutely certain there's nothing you know that could be useful to us in striking a deal with your father?"

"I know his favorite thing is money. And power. Give him either of those if you need him to do something for you and he might agree to your deal if he doesn't have a better offer. He might put up a fight about it to try to get more out of you, but he'll agree in the end."

"That's not exactly what I was thinking," Luca said. "What we need is something we can threaten him with. Threats always work better than promises at keeping someone in line."

"What about parties? Or dinners?" Enzo asked me. "He must've taken you out with him on occasion to show you off if he was hoping to marry you off to one of his business associates."

I thought back. My father *had* taken me to a few dinners once I became of age, nothing so big that I'd have a chance to wander away on my own. I tried to think if there were any names I could remember who'd also attended those get togethers. Particularly anyone who had appeared to be working with my father. Again, I shook my head. "He dressed me up and took me out sometimes, but nothing too elaborate. Just small dinners."

Luca and Enzo exchanged a look.

"I was usually the only woman there."

"Did these dinners consist of other mafia men?" Luca asked.

"Not always. Sometimes there were politicians or other city leaders." I twisted my hands in my lap as I tried to think. "I'm sorry, I never really followed that stuff. I don't remember their names."

"Let me try something," Enzo said. "Luca, may I borrow your laptop?" When his boss gave him the go-ahead, Enzo got up and took it from the desk and brought it over to where we were sitting. With a few taps on the keyboard, he brought up some photos of city officials in the Dallas area. He set the laptop on the table in front of me. "Do you recognize anyone here?"

I leaned forward and studied the faces in front of me. "This one." I pointed to a picture in the top row on the far right, then one farther down on the screen. "And this one."

"Good girl." Enzo turned the laptop around and showed Luca the two men I'd pointed out.

"Excellent," he told me. "Thank you, Sera. This is just what we were looking for."

He spent the next hour showing me more photos and grilling me on any small details I could remember. I told him everything I could, even if it was something as minor as to who sat next to each other and who appeared to be in a good or bad mood when they left, including my father.

When I couldn't think of anything else, he sat back, a thoughtful expression on his handsome face.

"As you know, Ciro knows we have you," Luca told me. "And Luigi, my father, has managed to somehow talk him into giving us a few days before we hand you back to him. We'll use those days to gather all of the information we can that would incriminate your father."

I felt like Luca wasn't telling me the whole story. "How did your father manage that?"

"I'm not sure," he told me.

Bullshit. Luca was the underboss. Of course, he knew. He didn't get as far as he had by being left in the dark. "I don't believe you."

He stilled in his chair and pierced me with those sharp, blue eyes. "It doesn't matter if you believe me or not, Sera. Just be grateful we have these days."

"I apologize," I told him immediately. "I was out of line. I'm just...nervous."

"Luca." There was a warning in Enzo's tone.

I immediately put my hand on his knee. "No. He's right. I shouldn't have questioned him." I turned back to the underboss, knowing he held my fate in his hands. "I am grateful for everything you've done for me."

He gave me a nod. "Let's move on, shall we?"

"Yes," I agreed.

Luca looked at Enzo. "Do you want her in here while we discuss this?"

His words rankled. What they were discussing involved me. My life. But I knew the rules in this world. And unfortunately, those rules didn't give a shit about me or my feelings.

"No. There's no need."

Luca got up from his chair and walked around his desk. "You may go, Sera," he told me as he took a seat. "Thank you for your help. I may need to ask you again in the coming days."

I got up to leave. I waited to feel the sense of disloyalty I should be feeling right now by telling my father's secrets to men who, if not his enemies, were definitely not his friends. Just a pinprick of guilt. Something. Anything.

But there was nothing.

"There's just one thing I need to warn you about," I told Luca.

Two sets of eyes turned my way. "What is that?" Luca asked.

"My father isn't exactly sane sometimes. He thinks he's much more powerful than he actually is. At least, that's the impression that I've always gotten."

"Thank you, Sera. I am aware."

I nodded, then allowed Enzo to take my arm and escort me out while Luca called Tristan and asked him to join them. When we reached the door, Enzo took my hand and brought it to his lips, pressing a kiss to my knuckles before lowering it to my side again, but he didn't let go.

"I'll come find you as soon as we're finished here."

"Okay."

"But first, give me back the pen that's in your pocket."

There was no condemnation in his eyes when they met mine. "I was nervous."

"I know."

Reaching into my back pocket, I handed it over, then I gave him a small smile. I left Luca's office with a slight glimmer of hope in my chest for the first time since Enzo had told me he knew who I was. Perhaps Veda was right.

Maybe they were coming up with a plan to free me from my father's prison.

I could only hope he would be smart enough to take the deal, or I had a very real fear this meeting would end up bloody.

CHAPTER 18

Enzo

When our meeting was over, I went searching for Sera. I'd gone through the entire upstairs before I began to panic. My heart raced and my hands shook as I rushed down the stairs, nearly running over Lisa in the process, who was heading upstairs with a pile of clean sheets in her arms. "Have you seen Sera?" I practically yelled at her.

"Yes." She smiled and pointed toward the patio doors. "She's enjoying the heated pool. I told her I'd get her a towel as soon as I made up the bed in Luca and Veda's room."

My head whipped around to the patio doors, and I could see ripples in the water at the end of the pool closest to the house. "I'll get her towel for her. But thank you."

"Of course." With another smile, she continued on her way.

In the laundry room, I opened the cabinet where Luca kept extra pool towels and grabbed one that was large and soft, white with blue stripes. Then I strode across the great room to the patio doors and quietly opened one and slipped outside.

My eyes found her right away, floating at the far end of the pool with her arms crossed beneath her chin on the side of the pool, staring out at the yellows and oranges and pinks of the setting sun that highlighted her pale skin. Her bright pink hair hung down her back, darkened by the water, and her legs kicked with lazy strokes beneath the water. I wished I could watch her all night. But darkness was coming, and the temperature was dropping. "I brought you a towel."

She gasped and spun around in the water, nearly sinking beneath the surface before she caught herself with one hand on the edge. "Enzo! You scared the hell out of me!"

I set the towel down in a chair and stuffed my hands into the front pockets of my slacks as I strolled over to her. "Are you ready to get out? Lisa will be starting dinner soon."

"No," she said. "This water is so warm it's like a giant bathtub." She hesitated, then said, "Why don't you come in with me?"

"I don't have a bathing suit."

She looked at me with an expression of complete innocence. "Neither do I."

My cock swelled at the thought of nothing touching her skin but the warm, silky water, even as anger heated my blood that she may have put on a show for anyone who could've been watching. The hypocrisy there didn't escape me, but at the moment, I didn't give a fuck. I glanced toward the glass doors, but no one lingered in the great room. "What are you fucking doing? What if someone saw you?"

"All the menfolk were locked away in Luca's office. The only ones who might've seen anything were Veda or Lisa. And they didn't."

"What about the soldiers patrolling the grounds?" I ground out.

Her gaze was challenging as she said, "It's nothing they haven't seen before."

"Sera." There was a strong warning in my tone. I was not in the mood.

She rolled her eyes and shrugged, one smooth, pale shoulder lifting from the water. "I don't think they can see up here. And if they can, well, they can consider it a bonus." A naughty grin spread across her face until it grew too wide, pulling the scrapes on her face. She winced, and the smile slipped away.

I lowered myself onto my haunches and pulled off my sunglasses, letting them dangle from my fingers. "Why are you fucking with me?"

"Because I can." She stared up at me defiantly, but as the seconds ticked by, the fire slowly faded from her eyes. "I'm sorry. I'm just feeling like...my life is out of my control again."

My anger faded with her confession. This was the last thing that I wanted. But I completely understood where she was coming from.

"Are you regretting what you told me earlier?"

"No," she said, but she didn't sound convinced. "If my only other option is going back to Ciro, I'd rather take my chances with you."

"I'm not sure whether to feel flattered or insulted."

"Same."

"Why do you say that?"

Her eyes met mine for a brief second before they danced away, and in the oncoming darkness, I couldn't read them.

"Sera?"

She gave me a forced smile. "Forget it. I'm getting cold. I think I am going to get out."

I rose to my feet. "One moment, please." Taking out my cell, I called in the order for all soldiers to make their way to the front of the house, where no wandering eyes would be able to see what was going on back here. Scanning the lake below, I didn't see any of our boats in the immediate vicinity, so I walked over and fetched her towel from the chair, leaving my sunglasses in its place, and making sure no one was in the house before I held it open for her.

Sera swam over to the ladder and quickly climbed out and into the waiting towel. I couldn't keep my eyes from traveling over her lush figure before I wrapped it around her, trapping her arms underneath. Then I pulled her against me, my breath leaving me on a deep sigh once she was safely in my embrace.

I thought she might pull away, but instead, she burrowed into my chest, soaking up my warmth. "Tell me about your family." Her voice was muffled in my suit jacket.

I immediately tensed. "My family? You've met my family. Luca, Veda, and Tristan are my family."

"Your wife and son," she clarified. "I'd like to hear about them."

The liquid heat that had been warming my blood the instant I felt her curves pressed against me froze in my veins. "It's cold, Sera," I said stiffly. "We should get inside."

"I'm not cold when I'm with you," she murmured. "And I want to stay out here for a while. I feel trapped in that house."

"It's only temporary," I assured her.

"I know." She sighed against me, and I pressed my lips to the top of her head. "So, tell me about your family."

Knowing I wouldn't get her off of the topic until I gave her something, I asked, "What do you want to know?"

"Everything. Where did you meet your wife? What was she like? What was your son like?"

"I met Alessandra when I was still in school. She was a year below me."

"So you were high school sweethearts?"

"No. We didn't start dating until I saw her again four years later. She started working at a store in our area." A store I was sent to by Luigi to collect our "fee" in exchange for our protection. "We started planning our wedding just a few months after we started dating, even though both of our families advised against it. But we were young and foolish and thought love would conquer all."

Sera leaned back to look up at me. "What was she like?"

I let my eyes travel over her perfect face. Not even the scratches from the tree bark could deter from it. "She was nothing at all like you," I admitted. "Ale wasn't from our world, and she didn't understand it, though she tried. At least at first." I paused, thinking back to when it all began to fall apart. "Over time, she started trying to convince me to leave. To get out. But I couldn't. Luigi wouldn't allow it. He needed me to stay with Luca."

I didn't tell her that I never actually tried to leave this life. It was the only life I knew. I wouldn't know how to survive without the family, especially Luca and Tristan. "She became bitter and anxious. Scared to go out. She was convinced Luigi had it out for her."

"Did he?"

That was a question I still asked myself. Back then, I'd told Alessandra she was being paranoid. That she was letting her imagination run away with her. But now? I honestly didn't know. But that wasn't something I needed her to worry about. "No," I told Sera. "He barely knew her." Not that that mattered. "But he didn't trust her because she was an outsider, as he put it."

I thought she was going to ask me more, like if it was true that I'd killed her, but then she changed the subject. "And what about your son?"

Elliot's dark curly hair, chubby face, and big, dark eyes flashed in front of my face. He was always a good boy, even when he was a baby. A happy boy. And he loved me. A love I wasn't sure I deserved. But as soon as he started walking, every time he saw me, he'd run to me and throw his little arms around my neck, even if I just stepped outside to make a call. I could still hear his giggles. And the way he begged me for "one more tickles" when I'd tuck him in at night, while his mother stood in the doorway and smiled.

"I'm sorry," Sera said, interrupting my memories. "You don't have to talk about him if it's too hard."

Glancing down at her, I was surprised to see tears in her eyes, and I wondered what it was she saw in my own. "He was a good boy," I said quietly. "Sweet. With dark curls and chubby cheeks." I watched, fascinated, as one of the tears escaped to run slowly down her cheek. "He was my whole world," I whispered, letting the pain wash over me. I didn't allow it to happen often, too afraid I would drown in it and never be able to fight my way up to the surface again.

She squeezed one arm up between us to cup my cheek in her palm, and I gripped it in my own, holding it there and turning my head to kiss the center, then the inside of her wrist, as the agony of losing my only child twisted and churned inside of me, gutting me alive until I lost my breath. The way it always did when I allowed myself to think about him.

"Enzo..."

I heard a similar pain in her voice. But I didn't want her to hurt. I didn't want to share this agony with her. Didn't want anything to dim the sunshine that radiated from her to warm my cold, dead heart. "Don't," I ordered. Releasing her hand, I wrapped my fingers in her wet hair and tugged her head back, bringing her lush mouth to mine. She tasted like tea and honey and I moaned, delving my tongue deeper into her sweetness.

Instantly, my cock grew hard. So hard I thought it was going to punch right through my slacks. I welcomed the distraction of her body as she pressed herself against me, needing somewhere to focus the pain before it suffocated me. Needing to release it.

Bending my knees, I wrapped one arm beneath her round ass and lifted her, breaking off the kiss as I looked around frantically for somewhere out of the view of the house. A covered seating area was off to my right where the roof of the house extended out to cover the deck. I took her over there as she clung to my neck and wrapped her legs around my hips.

There were no cushions on the chairs as Texas was heading into the cold season, but I barely felt the chill in the air as I pressed her against the side of the house, careful to keep the thick towel between her and the stone. I felt nothing but the heat of her body warming my cold soul. As soon as we were out of sight, I reached between us and freed my cock from my pants and buried myself inside of her, crying out against her shoulder when her wet pussy gripped me tight.

"Oh, god...Enzo..."

I took her hard and fast, right there against the house, our faces tucked against each other's shoulders to muffle the sounds we made until I bucked against her, my orgasm hitting me like a fucking earthquake. I emptied myself inside of her, then dropped to my knees, draping one of her legs over my shoulder to open her wide and putting my mouth on her. I could taste my semen and her desire as I found her clit with my tongue and slid two fingers inside of her, curling them until I found the spot that drove her wild.

Within seconds, Sera's fingers tightened in my hair as her entire body tensed and she came with hard pulses of her inner muscles, drenching my fingers even more, her breathy cries making me hard again.

She moaned as I slowly pulled my fingers out and licked them clean. Then I kissed the inside of her thigh, feeling the abrasions beneath my hand and kissing them, too. I looked up, hoping she could see the apology in my eyes.

She stood over me with parted lips, the towel draping open, revealing her soft belly, full breasts, and hardened nipples that rose and fell with every ragged breath, the expression on her face one I wanted to see every fucking day.

There was so much I wanted to say. But none of it would matter. Not now.

A small gust of cold air blew over us and goosebumps spread across her smooth skin. I immediately stood and pulled the towel closed around her again, then tucked myself back into my pants. "Come on." Tucking her against my side, I led her into the house. The smell of

Italian sausage and tomato sauce hit my nose and made my stomach grumble as we hurried across the great room and up the stairs. Amazingly, we managed to get inside our room with the door closed before anyone saw us.

Grabbing her hand as she tried to walk away, I told her, "I need to tell you something."

She looked down at my hand gripping hers and then up at me with a questioning look on her face.

"I just wanted to tell you I'm sorry for being so caught up in my own shit last night that I failed to notice I was hurting you." I brought her hand to my lips and kissed her knuckles. "It won't happen again."

"Stop apologizing. You didn't hurt me, Enzo. The tree did." Though her words were teasing, there was no amusement in her eyes.

But I wouldn't apologize for taking her in front of my men. She needed to learn that what she had done—running from me the way she had—was not acceptable. I stepped in front of her and pressed my forehead to hers. "I would do anything for you, Serafina. But I cannot allow you to disrespect me in front of my men."

"I wasn't disrespecting you. I was saving myself."

I will save you, I promised silently.

I'll save us both.

LOVE ALL ANIMALS

CHAPTER 19

Serafina

The day of our meeting with my father arrived.

I wasn't ready.

Enzo knocked on the bathroom door. "Sera? Are you alright?"

"No," I called. I was terrified. "Not really. But I'll be out in a minute."

"I'll be downstairs with Luca. Come to his office when you come down. We need to leave in twenty minutes. And Sera?"

I turned to face the door. "Yeah?"

It was so quiet that at first, I thought he'd changed his mind about whatever he was going to say. And then, in a low voice he said, "It will be okay, baby girl."

I listened to his footsteps as he crossed the room, and then I heard the bedroom door softly close. When he was gone, I lowered myself onto the side of the tub and dropped my head into my hands.

This was so damn crazy. Enzo hadn't told me what happened in Luca's office after I'd left, and I'd been too afraid to ask. But...but they had to have a plan to free me from my father. Right? Why else would he tell me it was going to be okay?

Right?

But as my mind raced over the possibilities, the small glimmer of hope that sparked inside of my chest was distinguished before it could catch flame. There was no way my father was going to agree to let me go. No matter what Luca threatened him with.

But what if he did? a small voice inside of me asked.

My heart skipped a beat at the thought of being free. What would I do? Would I leave? Or would I stay here with Enzo? Would he *make* me stay? I didn't know if I was ready for that either. But I had to admit, it was way better than the alternative. At least this way, I felt like I was given somewhat of a choice. I mean, I agreed to basically be his mistress for an undetermined amount of time of my own free will. And if I had to be under a man's protection, I'd much rather be with a man I already knew—quite intimately, I might add—than have to marry someone my father chose for me. A man who could be old enough to be my grandfather. A man who might beat me and loan me out to his friends. Or worse.

Taking a deep breath in a useless effort to calm my nerves, I stood and walked over to the sink to splash some cold water on my face and pat it dry with a small hand towel. Then I looked at myself in the mirror. I was pale, and there were dark circles under my eyes from not sleeping last night. Pulling out my makeup bag, I did what I could to make myself presentable.

In deference to my father and hopefully to help me gain favor in his eyes, I wore the dress Enzo had bought me that first night I showed up at his door. Luckily, the rain hadn't ruined it. I smoothed down the creamy lace, even though there wasn't a wrinkle to be seen, and checked my hair one last time. I'd pulled it back into a neat twist on the back of my head, leaving a few wavy strands to frame my face.

My father would hate the color, but there wasn't much I could do about it now. I'd thought about changing it back, but I liked it this way. And so did Enzo.

Bracing myself, I left the sanctuary of the bathroom, got my coat from the closet, and made my way downstairs, carrying my shoes. I'd put them on right before we left and save my feet from having to walk in heels any longer than I absolutely had to.

I found Enzo in the hallway outside of Luca's office. He had his back to me, and his cell phone was at his ear. He didn't hear me walk up, so I stopped and waited for him to get done with his conversation. His posture was stiff, and his fist was clenched at his side.

"Yes," I heard him say in a carefully controlled tone. "I understand."

A few seconds later, he ended the call. But instead of sliding his phone into his jacket pocket and going back into Luca's office, he stood there in the hall with his arms hanging at his sides. I could see the tension in his back and the way he gripped his phone like he was fighting the urge to smash it against the wall. "Enzo? Is everything okay?"

At the sound of my voice, he whipped around to face me. "Hey," he said. Then he looked down at the floor for a moment. When he raised his head again, he was once again cool and calm. "I apologize for my rudeness. I didn't realize you were waiting there."

I searched his face for some hint of what had just happened, but he had his sunglasses on, and I couldn't read him. "No. I'm sorry. I didn't mean to sneak up on you. I just didn't want to interrupt."

He gave me a tight smile. "It's fine." Opening his black jacket, he slipped his cell phone into the inner pocket. "You look lovely."

"Thank you." I tried to smile, and failed. "I'm scared shitless."

If I was hoping for him to give me a hug and tell me again that everything was going to be all right, I was horribly mistaken. Instead, he kept his distance. And I felt the first tingle of unease slither down my spine. "There's no need to be," he told me.

Something in his tone made my blood run cold. "Enzo? What's going on?"

He did come to me then. Taking me in his arms—coat, shoes, and all—he held me tight for a moment before he dropped a kiss on the top of my head. "Nothing is going on," he said. "We need to get going. Let me see if Luca is ready."

He left me standing alone in the hall, but didn't close the door behind him, so I was able to hear what was being said when he walked in. Like me, Luca knew right away that something was wrong. Enzo mumbled a response that I couldn't make out, but it seemed to placate Luca, for he didn't ask him anything else. The three men filed out of Luca's office and joined me in the hall. Tristan gave me a respectful nod and left to pull the SUV around to the front of the house. I shivered as he passed close to me.

"Hello, Sera," Luca said. "You look lovely."

"Thank you," I told him, but the words came automatically. I was way too worried and distracted to comprehend his compliment.

"Are you both ready?"

Enzo glanced at me. "We're ready. Let's go." Placing his hand on the small of my back, he escorted me to the front door, stopping only long enough for me to slip on my heels and my black coat before we went outside.

The ride to our meeting with Ciro was quiet, the tension inside of the vehicle so thick I was having a hard time breathing. Or maybe that was just me, panicking. Enzo and I shared the backseat, but every time I glanced his way, he was staring out the window. I told myself he was only being vigilant, as he always was, scanning the area around us for any signs of danger to him or his boss. But somehow, this time, I felt it was more than that, which only worried me more. Reaching across the leather seat, I took his hand and held on tight. He squeezed my fingers without looking at me, and wouldn't let me go when I tried to take my hand back.

It seemed to take forever, and yet no time at all, to get to Luca's club where the meeting was to be held in a private room upstairs. When we walked in, I saw girls earning their tips onstage in various stages of undress. None of the customers watching them paid any attention to us at all, their eyes riveted to the bare breasts and shaking asses that, if they tipped enough, they might actually get to take into a back room where they could get a much more up close and personal experience. At least, that's what Jade told me one time when we were chatting around the kitchen table, and I told her I'd never been to a strip bar.

As I looked around, I recognized three...no, four...of the faces crowding around the stage. Taking Enzo's hand, I tugged on it to get his attention. "My father has four men planted in the club that I can see."

He scanned the room. "Where?"

I gave him their description and told him their location. When we got to the elevator, he relayed the information to Luca.

"So your father isn't a complete idiot," he responded. "Thank you, Sera."

"They'll report to him how many of you there are." I knew he would know this, but I couldn't help but worry that we were walking into a trap.

But Luca smiled at me. "This is my club. It's smart of your father to have men here ready to go. However, as I said, this is *my* club. And I was prepared for this. There's nothing to worry about."

Easier said than done, but I would have to take his word for it.

The elevator doors opened to a large room easily half the size of the entire downstairs. Two chairs sat on either side of the entrance, empty of the guards who would normally sit there, and at the far end was a long wooden table that would easily sit twelve people with comfortable black leather chairs. Other than that, the room was empty.

Music pulsed through the floor as Luca led the way to the table and sat at one end, but wasn't so loud that you wouldn't be able to talk. Tristan took a place behind him and slightly to his right, placing himself between Luca and the elevator doors, while Enzo held out a chair for me on his left. Once I was seated, he sat on my other side. No sooner had we all sat down than the elevator doors opened and two of Luca's guards took up their positions on either side of them.

And then we waited.

Five minutes after the meeting was supposed to start, my father walked in. And he wasn't alone. Five of his closest men were with him. One more than what I knew was the agreed upon number. Luca had four men. My father should also have four men.

It was a matter of honor and a complete show of disrespect to the underboss. Tristan leaned down to Luca's ear, and I heard him ask, "What do you want to do?"

"Let it go," he responded. "For now. We'll see what he does."

With a nod, Tristan straightened to his full height and resumed his place, his dark eyes cold and hard as they assessed my father.

"Fina!"

My heart skipped the moment I heard that hated nickname.

"I've been so worried about you!"

His fake display of concern would've been funny if not for the circumstances. I watched as my father's hefty weight waddled across the space between us, but I made no move to get up to greet him, even if Enzo hadn't placed his hand over my arm in a show of keeping me in my seat.

When he reached the table, Luca stood up. "Ciro, it's good to finally meet you face to face. Please, have a seat." Though his tone was polite, there was a thin thread of anger made obvious in the clipped sound of the words and the lack of a handshake.

My father, who a lot of things but stupid wasn't one of them, sized up the situation and then dipped his head in apology. "Luca. You'll forgive me for my precautions and my late arrival, please. I was held up by traffic getting here." It wasn't a question. It was an order. My idiot father was giving *an order* to the underboss of the Italian mafia.

Surely, he had a death wish.

Luca's gaze never wavered as the temperature in the room seemed to drop thirty degrees. "And you'll forgive *me* for calling this meeting short, since it's quite obvious you don't know how to adhere to an agreement, verbal or otherwise, so I see no reason why I should waste my time with you any longer." Taking his cell phone out of his pocket, he never took his eyes off of my father as he tapped the screen and brought it to his ear. "Please send someone up to escort Ciro and his men out of the building. And while you're at it, remove the rest of his men from the club, by force if necessary, and tell the girls to keep the tips."

My father held up his hands. "Whoa, whoa. Wait. Please," he added.

Luca raised one eyebrow in question.

Visibly sucking up his pride, my father inclined his head. "Please accept my sincere apology, Luca, for this show of disrespect. I was playing on the side of caution, as this is my daughter's life on the line. Surely, you cannot blame me for that." When Luca only continued to stare at him, Ciro snapped his fingers at his nearest guard. "You. Wait for us downstairs in the car." The man nodded and did as my father asked.

As I said, my father wasn't a stupid man. Pompous, violent, and self-serving? Absolutely. But stupid? No.

When he was in the elevator, Luca said into the phone, "Disregard my last order. There is one man coming down. Please ensure he and the others in the club wait outside." He paused. "Thank you." Ending the call, he indicated a chair across from Enzo and I. "Please, Ciro. Sit. And let's start again."

When my father and his remaining men were in their chairs, Luca resumed his own seat. "Would you like something to drink? I can have it brought up from the bar."

"No, thank you," my father said. His deep-set eyes swung my way. "Fina, are you alright?"

"I'm fine," I told him. Enzo's hand tightened on my arm.

Not missing the possessive hold Enzo had on me, my father's hazel eyes grew cold. "I'm glad you haven't been...harmed."

Although the words were spoken like a concerned father, I heard the undertone of truth. My stomach twisted, and I averted my eyes to look more closely at his men. My blood froze when I met the eyes of the man sitting to his right. He wasn't one of my father's soldiers. He was his doctor. The same doctor who'd been periodically examining me for years to ensure my father that my virginity remained intact.

Why did he bring him *here*?

"Your daughter has not been harmed while under my care. You have my word. She was treated only as a respected guest."

Ciro leaned back in his chair and laced his fingers together over his stomach as he once again made it a point to notice Enzo's hand on my arm. "I do wonder, Luca, why it took you so long to set up this meeting when—

from what your father, Luigi, told me—Fina was found and brought to your home nearly a week ago."

His tone was underlaid with a challenge, but Luca only said, "I was tied up for a few days with business matters. I'm sure you understand." Luca's blue eyes glinted with a challenge of their own.

An undercurrent of tension came over the table, until my father smiled and said, "Of course. These things happen. I'm grateful to Luigi for letting me know my Fina was alive and well until we could arrange this meeting, and if there is anything I can do to show my gratitude, you only need ask."

My nerves were on edge as they finished up with the formalities and I waited to see what kind of deal Luca would offer my father for my freedom. Would he threaten his business if he didn't let me go? His life? I looked at the man who had raised me for most of my life and felt nothing. Well, almost nothing. He was still my flesh and blood, and I truly hoped his wouldn't be spilled here today.

I was pulled violently from my thoughts when Luca spoke. "I would like your loyalty, Ciro."

My father unlaced his fingers and spread his hands apart. "And you have it. Your father has been a friend of mine for many years."

That was something I hadn't known. Luca glanced at me, and I could only return his look of surprise.

"Not my father," Luca told him. "To me."

The room went completely silent as the true meaning of what Luca was saying became clear. But just in case there was any confusion, Luca clarified, "My father is no longer fit to hold the position he does within the family. I will be taking over that position as soon as I have the full support of the family. Not only here in Austin, but in the surrounding areas. Do I have that support from you, Ciro?"

The blood drained from my face as I finally understood what was happening. Luca was going to give me back to my father. And in return, he wanted my father's sworn loyalty to him and only him.

LOVE ALL ANIMAL

CHAPTER 20

Serafina

Holy shit.

I started to shake my head, pushing back on my chair to get up. To leave. But Enzo's hand left my arm and gripped the back of my neck like a steel vice so not only couldn't I get up from the table, but I also couldn't look at him.

I pushed down the panic and tried to think. If Luigi and my father were such long friends, perhaps he wouldn't go for the deal. It wouldn't surprise me. I spoke up. "Daddy, you don't have to do this. I'm a grown woman. I can take care of myself."

His attention remained on Luca as though I hadn't even spoken, and I could practically see the wheels turning in his brain. Friend or no, my father wanted to be on the winning side. His loyalty easily bought or sold. And his next words proved me right.

"And the rest of the family approves of this? How many do you have on your side?"

"Enough," Luca told him. "But it would be careless of me to get cocky. And one thing I never am is careless. I also know my father won't give up his throne easily, and I would like to feel confident about who is on my side and who is not."

Ever one for dramatics, my father made a show of thinking about Luca's offer. Luca allowed him his moment with an air of patience I didn't share.

Finally, my father shifted his eyes over to me. They traveled over my hair, and I could see the disapproval before they made their way to my face, then lower, to where Enzo held the back of my neck in a death grip. He turned back to Luca. "I will need to know that my daughter has not been raped while in your care. Her virginity must be intact, or she is worthless to me."

I nearly laughed hearing him say the words out loud, even as I blinked back tears.

But Luca wasn't fazed. "I can assure you, she has been treated with nothing but respect."

"I would like to take your word for it, Luca, but she was also on her own for weeks before she was found. Who knows what could have happened to her?" His eyes went to my hair again. "Luigi told me she was working in a club much like this one."

"I wasn't stripping," I burst out. "Jesus, Daddy."

His hand slammed down on the table, and I jumped. "You do not speak to your father like that."

Even though there was three feet of wood between us and I was flanked on either side by Luca and Enzo, fear shot through me. "I'm sorry," I told him. "I worked in a club. It wasn't a strip club." I didn't tell him that most of my customers were professional escorts and their dates.

Ciro waved away my argument and turned back to Luca. "I brought her doctor. He will examine her here before we talk any more of deals and loyalty."

"He will not," Luca told him. "Your daughter is now as she was when she came to my home. If you would like her returned to you, then I need your word that when the time comes, you and your men will stand behind me."

"I'm afraid I must insist."

Luca was about to refuse again when it occurred to me that this was the way I would be freed. Once my father's physician confirmed I was no longer a virgin, I would no longer have any value in his eyes. And Luca would just have to find another way to get my father over to his side. The war between him and his father wasn't my fucking problem. "It's okay. The doctor can examine me."

"NO." The angry response was from Enzo, who had been completely silent up until now. "You will not do such a thing to your daughter, here, in front of all of these men."

Ciro watched Enzo carefully as he told him, "These men have already seen my daughter's cunt. Plenty of times. Who do you think holds her down while the doctor examines her?"

If Enzo hadn't been wearing his sunglasses, and judging by the way he practically vibrated with rage beside me, I was fairly sure that my father would combust into flames without that barrier between them.

While he was distracted, I tried to shake off his hand, but he only tightened it, effectively holding me in my chair. I knew better than to look to Luca for help. He knew as well as Enzo did that if the doctor was allowed to check me, there would be no reason for my father to pledge his loyalty to him. So, instead, I kept my attention on my father.

Luca tried once more to talk him out of doing this. "Ciro, you have my word that nothing happened to your daughter while she was under my protection. There is no need to humiliate her like this."

"So you are certain that my Fina is still innocent?" my father asked him.

"Yes," Luca lied. No one mentioned what had happened to me in Mexico, and I was grateful. If my father discovered I'd "whored" myself out...

I shuddered. I couldn't even imagine what he would do to me. It wouldn't matter to him one bit that it had been completely against my will.

"Good," my father responded. "Then you have nothing to worry about when Dr. Ferrari examines her." He nodded to the man on his right. "Doctor, if you please."

The doctor stood up. As soon as he did so, Enzo came to his feet. "This is NOT happening," Enzo growled.

"Enzo. Stand down." Luca rose from his chair, buttoning his jacket as he did so, and left with no other choice without risking his own honor, said to my father, "If it will ease your mind to have Serafina examined, then by all means, do so." With one look, he ordered Enzo to release me.

At first, I thought he was going to disobey Luca's order. But then the pressure of his fingers left the back of my neck and Enzo's chair scraped the floor as he pushed it back and walked behind me to join Luca and Tristan.

Behind Luca, Enzo stood with his fists clenched at his sides and his eyes locked onto my father, but he said nothing more. I watched as a muscle jumped in his jaw, and I didn't understand why he was so angry. Yes, by doing this it would ruin Luca's original plan to get my father on his side, but he was easily bought. Another opportunity would come up. And this way, we could be together.

Unless he didn't want me.

My father, noticing his reaction, smiled. "Boys, get Fina on the table and hold her still."

I stood up. "That's not necessary, Daddy." With my head held high, I walked down to the end of the table where Dr. Ferrari waited. I hopped up onto the table and laid back.

As soon as I did so, two of my father's men came around to either side and held my shoulders down. I didn't fight them. There was no point. The skirt of my dress was shoved up to my hips and my underwear pulled down and off. I stared up at the ceiling, just wishing the whole ordeal to be over. Through the roaring in my ears, I heard the doctor tell my father's men to open me wider, and two hands grabbed the inside of my knees and spread my legs. Cool air caressed my exposed vagina and then two fingers were roughly shoved inside of me.

I gritted my teeth against the pain of him invading my body when I was tense and dry. I felt him pause, and then he pushed them deeper, feeling around until I thought his entire fist would soon be inside of me.

He pulled his fingers out and I was released. Shoving down my dress, I sat up on the table and scooted off the edge before I found my underwear and, with my back to everyone in the room, pulled them on quickly before fixing my skirt again.

Mortified, I stayed where I was and wrapped my arms around myself.

"Well?" I heard my father ask.

"Your daughter is no longer a virgin." The damn doctor—if that's what he really was—sounded strangely pleased about this fact.

Ciro's crazed eyes turned to Enzo. "It was you. *You* did this. You ruined my daughter." He slammed his beefy fist down onto the table.

Enzo stood still as a statue beside Luca and said nothing at all.

"Ciro." Luca's tone demanded compliance as he tried to take my father's attention away from Enzo and back to the matter at hand.

Reluctantly, my father dragged his eyes away from Enzo. "He raped my daughter." One fat finger jabbed the air in Enzo's direction. "He raped her and ruined her for any other man."

My own embarrassment forgotten, I threw my arms in the air. "For God's sake, Daddy! No one raped me!"

Furious eyes swung my way. "Then you allowed him to do this? You whored yourself out to him just like your mother? Who else here has fucked you?"

I shook my head, and I couldn't keep the contempt from my voice when I asked, "What does it matter?"

He turned back to Luca. "I demand that you marry her. He is your man. I demand that you restore my daughter's honor and the respect of the family by making an honest woman of her."

Oh, my god. A maniacal laugh rose within me, and I had to press my lips together to keep it inside. So *this* was his game.

But Luca didn't even crack a smile. "I cannot marry your daughter, Ciro."

"Your father might disagree with you when I call him to tell him what happened to my daughter while under your *protection*."

"My father does not run my life," Luca countered. He did not bring up Veda, and I didn't blame him. If my father found out about her, he would use it to his own advantage.

I expected him to push it further, but something in Luca's expression must've told him it would be of no use. "Fine," he said. "Then I demand *he* marry her." He indicated Enzo with a lift of his chin, crossing his arms over his ample chest in a gesture of stubbornness I knew well.

My heart sped up until it was racing so fast, I had to grip the back of a chair.

"Who Enzo marries or does not marry is entirely up to him," Luca told him.

My father turned to Enzo. "Well? What is your answer?"

Enzo hadn't moved or said a word since I was examined in front of everyone. But now, he looked at me down the length of the table. Even though I'd originally wanted nothing but my freedom, I couldn't stop the flood of hope from rising in my chest that he would agree to this. Hope that surprised me as much as it did him when he saw it on my face.

As I watched, something changed with him. Something that made my heart drop into my stomach. So subtle that I doubted anyone else would have noticed. But I did.

He turned back to my father. "No," he told him. "I will not."

My father's face turned blood red, and his eyes bulged beneath his heavy brows. Before I knew what was happening, he reached over to the man beside him, yanked his gun out of its holster, and pointed it at Enzo. "You will marry my daughter, or I'll shoot you right fucking here."

CHAPTER 21

Enzo

Slowly, I reached up and removed my sunglasses from my face. It was a risk to remove that barrier and allow this man to see me. *Really* see me. I couldn't allow him to see the pain immobilizing my limbs. The heartbreak cracking open my chest. I needed to be cold. Distant. Unfeeling. And if I pulled this off, it would be the greatest fucking performance of my life.

The barrel of the nine-millimeter rose a notch until it was pointed directly at the center of my forehead. Dust motes danced in the sunshine streaming in from the single high window on my left, and the muted sounds of techno music rose up through the floorboards from downstairs. Otherwise, the room was completely still and silent.

I watched them drift through the air for a moment before I refocused on the piece of shit holding that gun. He narrowed his eyes on mine, trying to put on a tough facade, but I saw the flash of uncertainty cross his jowled face when he noticed no fear staring back at him. After all, what did I have to be afraid of? Death? I wasn't afraid of death.

I was more afraid of being the only one left alive.

He stepped closer until I could smell the stench of spicy sausage oozing from his pores and hear the labored breaths fighting to put air into his lungs as he tried to contain his temper.

I sighed heavily at his dramatics, and once again told him my answer to his ultimatum. "My answer is no. I suggest you come to terms with it before things get ugly. For you."

From the corner of my eye, I saw Luca raise his hand, indicating for him to lower the gun as he stepped closer to me. Ciro did not follow his directive. "Enzo," he said in a low voice meant for my ears only. "Think about this."

Never taking my eyes from the man in front of me, I told him, "No. I'm finished with her, and we'll have no need for her after today. I'm not going to let this mezzo di merda, *this piece of shit*, bully me into marrying his daughter so he can run around bragging that he conned you into it." Then louder, "*I don't want her.*" I emphasized my words so there would be no confusion. The conviction in my voice rang clearly through the lies falling off my tongue, echoing off the bare walls of the clubroom where we had agreed to meet this fucking *stronzo.*

A strangled sob sounded to my left, and every muscle in my body ached with the effort not to look at the "her" I spoke of, or to acknowledge her in any way. Because if I did, this day wouldn't end well for either of us. I was taking a huge risk by sending her back to her father, but this was the only way to keep her safe…

From me.

I saw the way she looked at me just now. The hope that lit up her perfect face and shone from her bright eyes. Hope for a happily ever after I could never give her.

"That's not what you were thinking when you fucked my Fina, stealing her innocence!" he roared. "Something she kept close to her as a gift for her future husband!"

I hated that nickname for her. It wasn't who she was.

"Father!" she cried. "Jesus Christ!"

In my peripheral vision, I saw her take a rapid step back as his head snapped to the side, nostrils flaring at her disrespect. She'd forgotten herself again. Forgotten who she was speaking to. I tensed, prepared to throw myself between his gun and his daughter. She knew better than to push him when he was like this. Italian men weren't known for their cool heads, and this particular man was from the old generation, the one who believed women should be seen but not heard. They had no say over their lives in his world. But though his hand began to shake, he managed to control himself enough to keep the weapon pointed at me.

I talked to distract him. "She's right," I told him. "Your daughter's innocence or lack thereof was her decision, not yours. Perhaps you don't have the hold over her you think you do." I paused, pretending to consider my words. "Still, you seem to feel she broke a promise to you. However, if there was a promise made, it was between you and her. And I'm not going to pay her debt to you with my life. Dead *or* alive."

As I'd hoped, his attention—and his rage—was now focused fully back on me. This guy was a fucking joke. He didn't give a fuck about his daughter's virtue, other than the fact that she wasn't worth as much to him now that it was gone. Any plans he'd had to barter her off to some disgusting old man with a little girl fetish in exchange for power and a higher position within the family was out the fucking window. But it did not make her any less of a prize. She deserved better than that life.

She deserved better than me.

"Enzo." Luca had that tone in his voice. The tone an underboss of *La Cosa Nostra* used when he wasn't going to take any more bullshit from me. The one that boded ill for anyone who didn't do exactly as he said. "You will do right by this girl. And we will discuss the terms of the marriage like gentlemen. This could still work to our advantage. We need everyone we can get on our side if I'm going to dethrone my father." He didn't bother to try to lower his voice. Luca was nothing if not straightforward. And making arrangements such as this was how things worked in our world. Very rarely did any kind of deal happen without it being advantageous for both parties involved.

"We don't need him," I argued without taking my eyes off the weapon pointed at me. "And I'm sorry, Luca. But I won't do this. There's no way in hell I'm marrying his whore of a daughter just because she thought fucking me would save her from having to spread her legs for the man her father chose for her. She's a rebellious brat whose plan didn't work out the way she thought it would. But that's not my problem."

Blocking out her muffled cry of pain I'd caused with the dagger of my words, I watched in amusement as her father's face, already red with anger, became mottled with purple. The hand that held the gun jerked, unable to lock down its aim on my face, and spittle sprayed my face as he roared with rage.

From the corner of my eye, I saw Luca take a step toward him, but he was too late. My ears rang as the gun went off. A fraction of a second later, a trail of fire burned along the left side of my face just below my eye. A woman's scream filled the air as everyone in the room froze.

I didn't so much as flinch as the bullet grazed my cheek. I just smiled, and put my sunglasses back on as Tristan tackled Ciro to the ground and Luca wrestled the gun away from him. But her father wasn't alone. He'd brought four of his own men along for our meeting, and they wasted no time jumping in on the fight to protect their boss. As did Luca's two soldiers who'd been watching the elevator doors.

The gun went skittering across the floor. Fixing my jacket, I walked over and picked it up. By the time I turned around again, Luca was on his feet with her father held up by the back of his neck and Tristan and our guards had his four soldiers against the wall with a gun in each hand pointed at their balls.

Much as I tried, I couldn't stop myself from running my eyes over her, just once, to make sure she was okay. Tears ran down her face and she took a step toward me before she remembered the things I'd just said and stopped, a look of utter betrayal and heartbreak on her pretty face.

Luca waited for me with my would-be murderer, one arm around his throat and the other holding his arm wrenched behind his back so high it was only a matter of time until his shoulder popped out of the socket.

Tucking the extra weapon into the front of my black slacks, I approached them. Rivulets of warm blood ran down my cheek and dripped onto my white button-down shirt as I stood silently before the man who had just tried to kill me.

His dark eyes burned with the rage of his chauvinistic ancestors as he stared me down. "You *will* honor my daughter," he ground out. "She was an innocent girl!"

I had to admire his balls. Even wrapped up in Luca's death hold, he managed to sound intimidating. I stepped closer, ignoring the icy fire in Luca's blue eyes that promised me a sound reprimand and maybe a go in the fighting ring when we got ourselves out of this. "I will not take a virgin whore as my wife. A woman who tricked me into this just to escape you and your tyranny."

"I did no such thing, you son of a bitch! And you know it!"

It took everything in me not to turn to her. Not to react. To keep my body relaxed and my face expressionless. It was only my eyes that ever gave me away, and it was why I always kept them hidden behind dark glasses.

My mother once told me that if it wasn't for what she could see behind my eyes, she would truly think I had no feelings at all. And because I'd loved her more than anyone, she was the only one I'd ever let see. The only one I'd ever let in until Luca and Tristan had taken me in.

Except I had let Sera in. I'd let her see. She *knew* me. And that was why it was so hard for her to accept this.

"Ciro, let me talk to Enzo," Luca said in her father's ear. "Call off your men and let me talk to him. I'm positive we can work something out." He emphasized the urgency of his request by shoving his arm up just a tad higher on his back.

The Italian curses that flew off Ciro's tongue were truly colorful as his eyes squeezed shut against the pain. After a few moments, he jerked his chin down in a nod.

"Are we good?" Luca asked him.

A grunt was his only answer. Luca took that as confirmation that he would do as he was told, and released the cocksucker from his chokehold before stepping away, fixing his jacket and pulling down the cuffs of his shirt as he did so. "Tristan," he called.

Tristan immediately lowered his weapons, turned, and rejoined us, as did our guards. Ciro's men peeled themselves off the wall and followed a bit more sullenly. Silently, we all went back to our original places, two groups of five facing each other across six feet of floor. Only this time, we held all of the firearms. The lady whose honor was in question watched us from her place of honor behind her father and his men and slightly to the left near the end of the table. However, I didn't have to look to know exactly where she was. I could feel her there, like a fucking black hole sucking me into her abyss against my will.

Ciro spoke first. "I'm not leaving here until we've agreed on retribution for my daughter. I'm demanding marriage, and I'll accept nothing else. It will repair her honor and save the reputation of my family. In return, as soon as the vows have been spoken, I will pledge my loyalty to you, Luca, and *only* you. After all, we will practically be family. This alliance between us will benefit us both, and I'm sure you wouldn't want to do anything to threaten that."

The implication was clear. If I didn't agree to this, he would turn the other factions against us.

For the first time since we'd arrived, I took my eyes from him and spoke to the man who, underneath all of this shit, was my closest friend. "I can't do this, Luca."

There was no hesitation from him. "I'm sorry, Enzo. But you must." He paused and took a breath, turning slightly toward me and speaking so softly only I could hear him. "I know where your head is, my friend. But you can't live your life afraid, Enzo. You have to agree to this arrangement, for yourself and for the good of the family."

My guts twisted, and my heart began to pound. To refuse his order would be a true test of his love. To see if my lifetime of friendship and loyalty meant more to him than his position in the family and his revenge against his father. I could save my sanity. I could watch as some other man took her as his wife and filled her belly with his children. Because it would happen. It didn't matter if she was no longer a virgin. One look at that face, one touch of her skin, one night with his cock inside that sweet pussy, and any man would be her slave for the rest of his natural life...and maybe beyond.

I clenched my shaking fists at my sides as a red haze of jealousy and fury edged the corners of my vision.

But the way I felt didn't matter.

That man would not be me.

That man could NOT be me.

"I can*not*."

Luca turned his back to Ciro completely. "Enzo, if you refuse him, it could start a war. One we cannot afford right now."

"Let him take her." Even as I said the words, every cell in my body screamed in pain. "Let him take her back. He's running drugs from Mexico. He's a competitor. We'll cut his supply lines and contaminate his product until he has no choice but to beg for your forgiveness."

Luca's blue eyes were filled with disbelief. "She will hate you."

Yes. She would.

I stepped around Luca. "I will not be forced into marrying your daughter. Go ahead and take her if you think you can get anything for her."

Unable to stay in that room with her a moment longer, I walked to the elevator and got inside.

But I couldn't resist one last look at her perfect, tear-stained face right before the elevator doors closed tight, as did the wall around my heart.

CHAPTER 22

Enzo

Sera had been gone for two weeks when we got the invitation in the mail for a Christmas Eve wedding.

I was in Luca's office going over some last-minute changes for a shipment we had coming in when Lisa brought it in to him. When he opened the envelope and saw the telltale stationary, he stopped. His blue eyes found mine as I rose from my chair and approached his desk.

"Go ahead," I told him.

The room blurred around me as he pulled out the invitation and opened it. "It's not her," he told me. I barely heard him over the blood rushing through my ears.

"It's for my father. 'You and a guest are cordially invited to the wedding of Luigi Morelli and his bride to be on December 24th...'" He didn't bother with the rest. "It's not her," he said again. "My father is marrying Linda." There was a note of disbelief in his voice, and I knew why. Luigi had never remarried after Luca's mother. He would move them in. Abuse them however he saw fit to punish them for not being the one he really wanted. But he never, ever married them.

Maybe he was starting to feel his age and decided what the hell. Or maybe Linda had somehow cracked open his cold heart. Either way, I didn't really care. What he did with his life was no concern of mine.

I sank back down onto the couch and scrubbed my face with my hands. I wasn't in the mood for a wedding. Or being around people. Or anything for that matter.

From what I'd been told by Luca and Tristan, after I left the meeting, Ciro commanded his men to grab Sera and took her with him back to Dallas. No one had any idea what he'd done to her after that. We assumed she was once again locked in her room as he tried to find someone who would take a slightly used bride.

The thought made me sick to my stomach. But she was better off away from me. I was getting far too attached. People died when I got too attached. And I thought that once she was gone, this crazy need I had to possess her would fade.

I was wrong.

Instead, it ate away at my insides until I couldn't eat. Couldn't sleep. I spent hours in the gym until I was so exhausted I could barely walk, and still I would go back to the hotel and lie there in bed with my eyes wide open, listening for the soft sounds of her breathing and hoping to catch the lingering scent of flowers and coconuts on my sheets, despite the fact that housecleaning had changed the linens while I was gone.

The only thing I had left of her was the money I'd locked away in my safe. I'd told her the truth when I said I wouldn't give it to her father. She'd worked hard to save up to start a better life, and I knew that, someday, I would get a phone call. My heart stuttered in my chest every time someone knocked on my door, only to be crushed again under the weight of disappointment when it wasn't her.

As the days went by, she never contacted me to demand I return her money. I never heard anything about her, and neither did Luca. There was nothing at all. It was like she'd never been here in my life, and I'd dreamed her gap-toothed smile and soft, soft skin.

"I suppose we have to make an appearance," Luca muttered as he stared down at the invite. "It would make my father even more suspicious if we didn't."

Which meant Tristan and I were required to attend also. Because there was no way in hell I was allowing Luca to walk into a room filled with his father's friends and supporters without my being there to help Tristan protect him and Veda.

Goddammit.

WE ARRIVED at Saint Mary Cathedral five minutes before the ceremony was supposed to start. Luigi's soon-to-be wife had chosen the largest, oldest, Catholic church in downtown Austin to say the vows that would ruin the rest of her life.

The church was beautiful in the way all old churches were. Victorian Gothic in structure and made entirely of limestone, with two bell towers, it was originally designed in the 1870s and renovated in the early 2000s. Inside, dark-stained Gothic arches rose high above our heads and stained-glass windows from France and Germany lined the walls. And of course, Jesus hung from the cross in a morbid display behind the candlelit alter to remind us of our many sins.

The wooden pews were already filled with guests as Luca, Veda, Tristan and I made our way to the front of the church where our seats were reserved in the front row. I sat beside Veda—stunning in a red, long-sleeved dress that hugged her figure and a soft, white wrap over her shoulders—and Tristan took his place beside Luca. Two more of Luca's men stood at the back, watching the crowd, who spoke in low murmurs as they waited for the show to start. And more were outside walking the perimeter, keeping an eye out not only for uninvited guests, but also on Luigi's men.

A door opened to the right of the altar and Luca's father came out, along with the priest dressed in full robes. He found us immediately, and he smiled before facing the back of the church.

I immediately became suspicious. Luigi and Luca's relationship had always been stormy. And since Mario, Luca's brother, had disappeared, they could barely be in the same room together.

Something was going on. And I had a feeling I wasn't going to like it.

But I had no time to talk to Luca as organ music filled the room, indicating the start of the ceremony. All of the guests went quiet and rose to their feet. I scanned the room as the doors at the back of the church opened and gasps were heard when they saw the bride. Tristan and I exchanged a look. Apparently, an overly expensive wedding dress could make anyone look good.

Over the heads of the crowd, I could see only the white poof of the top of the wedding veil. My eyes skimmed over the man walking her down the aisle, only the top half of his head visible, before moving on.

Something struck me as odd, and my heart began to race inside my chest before I fully comprehended what I'd just seen.

No.

It couldn't be.

The father and daughter couple approached the front of the church with agonizing slowness. My eyes were glued to the spot they would appear. The seconds ticked by as the notes from the organ seemed to grow louder, mocking me.

A piece of a white gown flashed before my eyes as the bride took a step. And another. More of the skirt was visible. The flowers. And then she was hidden by the girth of the man beside her until they arrived at the altar where Luca's father waited with the priest.

The man and his daughter stopped, his back to me, hiding her from my view. I tried to slow my breathing as his arms rose and he lifted the veil over her head, then bent down to give her a kiss. Ever the proud father. So full of himself to make such a match for his only daughter. He stepped aside, leaving her there with her groom, and for just a moment, her blue-gray eyes locked onto mine before she turned to face Luigi. A vision in white, she wore very little jewelry other than the silver nose ring and diamonds in her ears, her pink hair the only color as it fell over her shoulders and back.

I heard Veda gasp beside me as everyone around us sat back down. Heard Luca quietly say my name.

And then there was nothing but red.

Keep reading with His Proposal. The final book in the His Possession Trilogy.

HIS
proposal
ANGEL RAYNE

Hi! My name is Angel Rayne and I write dark, delicious romance with antiheroes who would burn down the world to save the woman they love. I never understood why the villains never win the girl, and so I decided to write them their own love stories where they do.

Here are a few other odds and ends about me...

-Music inspires my stories and I make playlists for every book.

-I am not a fast writer. My stories take time to write. They need to brew in my head. To have book releases close together I have to write ahead. But I would much rather take the time the stories need to be the best they can be than try to rush them out. Trust me on this one.

-I love the rain, and I'm happiest when I'm sitting in a coffee shop with my laptop as it storms outside.

-I prefer to go watch movies alone, with one of those fancy coffees hidden in my purse. (Yes, I really do this.)

-My husband calls me his "little bird" because anything that sparkles catches my eye.

-I will never have enough soft blankets. Ever.

-I love ALL THE DRAMA...but only in books.

-I will forever re-watch The Phantom of the Opera with the hope that by some miracle, this time Christine will choose the right guy.

Thank you for reading my stories, and I always love to hear from you! You can reach me at: angel@angelrayne.com